PLAYING HARD
By A K Love

Playing Hard
Copyright © 2017 by Author A.K Love. All rights reserved.

amandaloveblog.com

www.facebook.com/a.love124/?ref=aymt_homepage_panel

Cover Art: Addendum Designs

This book is dedicated to Jane – for giving me Tinkerbell on the rocks.

PROLOGUE

The loud banging from the front door makes me jump and I almost spill my soda down my t-shirt. I hesitate in the kitchen, not wanting to answer the door, but frightened not to in case it sets Dad off. His moods are so unpredictable and most days Mom and I have to tread carefully around him.

I sigh as the banging intensifies, accompanied by a man's angry voice outside. I'm still debating what to do when Dad finally drags his ass off the sofa, muttering under his breath as he answers the door.

I start to make my escape upstairs but falter in mid-flight as a man pushes his way angrily through the door and into the house.

The intruder has a swarthy complexion, his greasy black hair flopping over one eye, dark stubble crawling up his neck and around his jaw and mouth. A shiver slithers down my spine as his eyes fall on me, his hot gaze roaming greedily up and down my body, making me wish I was wearing more than the shorts and t-shirt I'd changed into when I got home from school.

"Go to your room, Prue."

Is that fear I hear in Dad's voice? I have no idea who this man is or what he's doing in our house but Dad seems to know him, and not in a good way, it seems.

I don't need any further prompting, not wanting the other man's eyes on me for a second longer. I turn and quickly continue up the stairs to the safety of my bedroom, closing the door firmly behind me. Dad never has visitors so I'm both surprised and unsettled as to who the man downstairs is.

For someone who's been out of work for as long as I can remember, Dad's hardly ever here. I don't know where he goes for most of the day and I'm pretty sure Mom doesn't either but it's a relief when he's gone, not to have to deal with his ever- shifting moods and unpredictable temper.

It's been hardest for Mom, living the sham that is her marriage and giving up her dream of a degree in counselling so she can hold down the two jobs that keep us afloat week to week, paying our bills by waitressing and a cleaning job at one of the local high schools. She's made so many sacrifices to keep a roof over our heads and clothes on my back. She's still young and she should be living her life to the full now instead of working herself into the ground.

I know she didn't want to give up on Dad and has fought so hard to keep us together but the idea of us being a normal family is a joke.

Mom says that Dad wasn't like he is now when they met. Dad was her high school sweetheart and she fell pregnant with me when she was seventeen. They decided that getting married was the right thing to do and things were okay until Dad lost his job. Then it all went to shit.

Dad fell into a depression and withdrew from life, from us, and years later we're all still suffering the consequences.

As soon as I'm eighteen I'm out of here and off to college and it can't come a day too soon. Five more years until I can make that a reality and it seems like an eternity.

I hope that then Mom will finally find the courage to leave herself, maybe even come with me so she can be close by while I'm at college. We could get a small apartment and we'd be happy, just her and me.

The mumble of voices drifts up the stairs, bringing me out of my thoughts and the discussion seems to be getting heated as the other man's voice becomes louder and angrier. I crack open my door, trying to make out what they're saying.

"...what the fuck you're playing at?"

"I'll pay it back, with interest, I promise." Dad sounds...scared!

"So, what you're telling me is, you been chasing the dragon with the boss's junk? The same junk you were supposed use for the drop off? You've already been warned once, you stupid prick!"

"I ... I just needed a little for myself. If you can just give me a few days ..." I can hear the pleading note in my Dad's voice and it makes me feel nauseous.

"So, let's say I give you your few days. What you gonna give me in return, eh?" The other man's voice has taken on a nasty edge.

"I got a little pineapple or, um, some... uh ...chocolate rock." I can hear the tremble in Dad's voice.

I have no idea what the two men are talking about but alarm bells are going off in my head as I listen, rooted to the spot by the door.

"I'm not talking about that you stupid fucking idiot! I'm talking 'bout a little virgin pussy."

"V ... virgin? I haven't... I mean ...I don't have..."

"Oh, but you do. And from what I've just seen that sweet pussy is just waitin' upstairs for me to fill it."

"What? No, no you can't! Just...shit! Put the knife down. Just give me a few days, please!"

My hand flies to my mouth and my stomach drops to the floor at my Dad's words.

"You know what? I'm feeling generous, so I'll give you those few days to make things square," the other man says.

I release the breath I wasn't aware I'd been holding.

"But, fact remains, you stole the boss's shit. Nobody steals his shit. So, now I'm gonna need a little down payment as a sign of good faith, you understand?"

I can't hear Dad's reply but I'm sure it wasn't anything good.

"So, this is how it's going to work. I'm gonna go upstairs and fuck your daughter bloody and you're going to stay down here like a good boy. You don't move, you don't make a sound. If I even hear you breathing too loud, I'll cut your fucking dick off and feed it to you. Now you learn there are consequences to your actions."

There's a pause and then the stairs creak with the sound of booted feet and my brain suddenly catches up with what I've just heard.

Shit! Oh, God! No, no, this can't be happening!

I'm suddenly galvanized into action as adrenaline kicks in, looking around my room desperately, my eyes landing on my second-hand oak desk with my homework scattered over the top. It's heavy, but I get my weight behind it and push with all my strength, sliding it in front of the door just as the door handle moves.

He pushes the door open and it bounces off the desk, leaving a small gap. His hand comes around the door and he shoves it hard, making the desk skid back like it weighs nothing at all and pushing his body through the gap. He's not a huge man, but I know without a doubt that he's still big enough to do some damage to me.

"Don't touch me!" I scream at him, backing up into the room as far as I can until my back hits the windowsill.

"Now, now, chica. Let's not make this any harder than it has to be." His tongue sweeps across his mouth as he moves toward me and the sheen of his saliva highlights the scar on his top lip.

I turn quickly, reaching for the window latch but he's on me, grabbing the back of my t-shirt and hauling me away from the window.

He wraps his hand around my throat from behind, squeezing my windpipe as he pins me back against his body and I whimper as I feel the blade of a knife against my ribs. The smell of stale cigarette smoke and rancid sweat infiltrates my nostrils, making the bile rise in my throat.

"Don't be trying to run from me, chica. You're going to like this. I'm gonna fuck you good and hard. Maybe then your daddy will think twice about stealing shit that doesn't belong to him."

He grinds his hips against my back and the hand that's gripping my throat moves down over my breasts and squeezes them roughly before heading down my stomach towards the waistband of my shorts.

"No!" I struggle against him, feeling the edge of the knife against my skin and suddenly, he bends his head to my neck, biting me hard.

I cry out in shock and pain, my brain unable to fathom what's happening. "You like it rough, don't ya chica?" His breathing is labored with the excitement of what he's about to do to me.

"Dad!" I scream. "Daddy, please!" I feel the darkness closing in around me and I know I'm going to pass out, relieved because it means I don't have to endure this living nightmare while I'm conscious.

The stench of his breath washes over my face, the grip of his hand against my body becomes punishing as I struggle against him.

"Daddy's not gonna help you, honey."

"No, but Momma is!"

"What the fuck?" He staggers back in surprise, releasing his hold on me and I turn to see Mom stood behind him holding a baseball bat. She's breathing hard and looks like an avenging angel - a very pissed one at that.

"Take your fucking hands off my daughter!" Momma forces the words through clenched teeth.

"Bitch! You think you can.... "

Mom swings the bat, aiming for his head, but he's too quick and intercepts it with his arm, sending it clattering to the floor.

"You're gonna regret that, you stupid fucking whore." He lunges at Mom and grabs a handful of her hair, using the leverage to twist her head back as he holds the knife to her throat.

"Get away from her!"

Without thinking, I grab the bat from where if fell on the floor and I swing it with every ounce of my strength. There's a sickening crack as the hard wood connects with the side of his head and he goes down like a sack of shit and doesn't move.

I'm breathing hard as the bat falls from my nerveless fingers, shock settling over me as my brain tries to figure out what has just happened.

Mom scoops me up in her arms and I cling to her, sobbing. "It's okay, baby, it's okay," She croons, stroking my hair. She tilts my face up to hers so she can look directly into my eyes, "Go pack a bag, quick as you can, honey. We're leaving."

PRUE

For the hundredth time, I tug on the neckline of the dress, trying to adjust it to cover a little more of my generous boobs where it dips into a deep V at the front. It's revealing more of my rounded flesh than I'm comfortable with but the white dress, blonde wig and bright red lipstick are all part of my costume tonight.

I'm not even sure why I'm here - it's not like I even know Carolyn that well. We met at the self-defence class we both attend and got chatting and the next thing I know I'd accepted her invite to her fancy-dress birthday party. At the time, it had sounded like a good idea - I don't often get the chance to go out and have a little fun, but now I'm just wanting to head home to my bed, which is calling me after a long day at work.

I'll stay just long enough to have a drink and show my face.

The party is already in full swing as I climb out of the cab and music blares from the open door and windows as people mill around out front, drinking beer and goofing around.

I make my way past Spiderman who's shooting "webs" at his friends from devices strapped to his wrists and as I approach the front door I notice Supergirl, obviously not feeling so super, as she vomits all over the flower beds. Classy.

I push my way through the throng of people lining the hallway and into the carnage that is Carolyn's birthday party.

The living area is packed with people dancing and drinking and couples making out in dark corners. The pervasive smell of sweat and pot is heavy in the air. My nose wrinkles in distaste, having more reason than most to hate those smells. A keg of beer sits on a stand next to the kitchen hatch and a group of guys dressed as ninja turtles are gathered around it downing shots.

"Prue, you came!"

I hear a familiar squeal behind me and turn to see Carolyn. She's a complete Disney nerd, so I'm not at all surprised to see her dressed as Tinkerbell, complete with gossamer wings and wand. "Hey, Carolyn. Sorry I'm late, I came straight from work. Happy birthday!"

"Thanks, Prue." Carolyn shoves a plastic cup of punch under my nose. "Here ya go! You got some catching up to do." I'm pretty sure Carolyn is already buzzed, judging by the way she's swaying on her feet and slurring her words. "Your get-up looks amazeballs by the way. You look hot as Marilyn Monroe, I almost didn't recognize you with the blonde wig!"

I take the cup from her and hold it up to my nose before taking a sip. The liquid burns a fiery trail down my throat and makes my eyes water. "There's a lot of people here," I cough, indicating the packed room around us.

"Yeah, my brother crashed the party with some of his friends," Carolyn replies, pointing at the ninja turtles by the beer keg who now appear to be trying to out-ninja each other. Or dancing – it's hard to tell.

"Hey, Carolyn!" Elvis appears behind her in a white jewelled one-piece slit to the waist with fake chest hair, "Maisie needs you – she's hurling up on the flower beds out front. I've been holding her hair up for the last five minutes but I think she may need to go home."

"Wunnerful!" Carolyn wobbles on her feet and sloshes some of her drink down the front of her outfit. "Mingle!" she instructs, spreading her arms wide to indicate the room at large as she's dragged off by Elvis.

This whole experience is becoming more surreal by the minute.

I take another swallow of my drink as I scope the room again, the liquid sliding down my throat a little easier this time. I'm feeling out of my element and the need for my bed is outweighing the need to party.

I drain the contents of the plastic cup – may as well enjoy a little nightcap before I leave - and pull out my cell to call a cab.

As I turn towards the door I don't see the puddle of beer on the floor and my feet skid out from underneath me.

I'm about to eat the ground in spectacular style when strong hands break my fall. Strong, *green* hands. I look up into a pair of chocolate brown eyes surrounded by a beautifully sculpted face which the green paint does nothing to disguise.

For a moment, it feels like we're suspended in time as I lose myself in the heat of his hands on my waist, his thumbs lingering just below my breasts and I can almost hear the *zap* of attraction that crackles in the air between us.

Before I can make sense of my overwhelming reaction, a pair of sensual lips come crashing down against my own and I'm being kissed senseless by none other than Shrek. And, by God, Shrek is a good kisser!

It takes me a full minute to realize that not only am I enjoying the kiss, I'm also kissing him back. At some point my hands

13

have tangled in his thick, dark hair as his tongue dances with mine. His mouth is making my whole body sing, making me want things.

Dirty things.

Filthy things.

Reality comes crashing down on me as I remember where we are and what I'm allowing him to do to me.

I wrench myself out of his arms, which is no mean feat considering the size of him. He's a mountain of a man and it seems his costume choice fits him in more ways than one.

"Get your fucking hands off me!" I'm breathing heavily as I give him my best death stare – the one that normally makes men turn and run in the opposite direction.

I'm not sure why I'm so angry. Or so turned on.

My stare doesn't have any effect on Shrek and he doesn't move, looking a little shaken himself as he holds his hands up in the universal sign of surrender.

"Whilst I appreciate your help, I would've appreciated it more if you'd kept your tongue in your own mouth!"

I turn on my heel, without mishap this time, and march toward the door. As I leave, I am definitely not thinking about the feel of his mouth on mine or the annoying throb between my legs.

Nope, not thinking about it at all.
☐

JAKE

Shit!

I watch as my blonde bombshell walks away, her back straight and her rounded ass swaying, making her skirt swish around her long legs. There's no way she can know that the feel of her soft curves against me has caused a reaction that hasn't occurred for months.

My dick went from zero to locked and loaded in two seconds flat and I couldn't help myself. Kissing her in that moment seemed as natural as taking my next breath. Those full red lips were begging for my mouth and I can't help but wonder how they'd feel wrapped around my now throbbing cock. Just the thought robs me of breath.

The white dress did nothing to disguise her hourglass figure and magnificent tits. Dear God, I was so capable in that moment I could've lifted her dress, slid her panties aside and buried myself in her heat right there and then!

My reaction is even more surprising because she's the exact opposite of my usual type of woman. I've always gone for blonde and tanned – or I did until my libido decided to go into early retirement six months ago.

I have no idea what her hair color is underneath the wig she was wearing but her lush curves are a direct contrast to my usual tastes, in the most delectable way.

I discreetly adjust the pants of my outfit and wonder again at the physical reaction she's just re-kindled. Who is this woman that's given my body a new lease of life? The urgency of that question diverts the blood from my dick back to my brain and I take off after her.

I head out the door and down the path in time to see a cab pulling away with my blonde bombshell in the back, her vivid green eyes looking back at me through the rear windscreen as the cab disappears into the night. Shit!

I go back inside, speaking to a few of the guests to see if anyone knows who she is, but no one remembers her. It's like she's a ghost – here one minute and gone the next. The only reminder of her is the twitch of my previously dormant cock when I remember her soft body against mine as we kissed.

Six months is a long time for a man to be dead from the waist down. In that time, I've gone from having an impressive one-eyed monster with a voracious appetite for pussy to a pathetic slow-worm with an inferiority complex.

I know it's my punishment for my man-ho ways after Monica and I split. That woman has done a number on me and I'm not sure I'll ever recover from her betrayal. I'll certainly never trust another woman again. I'd loved her, was going to marry her, believed she was having our baby.

All lies.

What a fucking gullible fool!

I fell for Monica the first time I saw her. She was beautiful, blonde and I wanted her. She was my first lover and I fell for her hard and deep.

The feeling seemed to be mutual because she was on top of me in my bed the very same day, giving me an education in the ways of a woman's body.

Things were good for a while, we got along well and seemed to have similar tastes and outlooks on life. When she told me she was pregnant after six months together, the news came as a complete shock as she'd told me she was on birth control.

Once the shock wore off I quickly came around to the idea of being a daddy and was even more excited when her belly started to grow with our baby. Asking her to marry me had seemed like the next step – call me old-fashioned but I wanted our baby to have my name.

Then it had all gone to shit.

I came home early from training one afternoon and found her fucking another man in our bed. Caught in the act. No way she could deny that one. There's nothing like the pain of seeing your pregnant fiancée grinding away on another man's cock. Or being told that the child you thought was yours isn't - that the real father is the man whose cock she was grinding on. She took great pleasure in screaming that little nugget of information at me as I threw them both out.

She also told me in no uncertain terms that she'd never loved me and how I'd never satisfied her – in and out of bed. She'd just liked the attention being with a pro football player had brought her. The effect of those words was devastating and how I kept my fists to myself I'll never know. Part of me knew even then, with the fury running through my bloodstream, that if I hadn't I'd be in a jail cell somewhere and she would have won.

So, instead, I smashed up the bed until it was nothing but firewood and moved to a new apartment the next day. I couldn't stay there with the smell of their sex and deceit hanging in the air.

Then I went on the biggest bender imaginable, trying to lose the pain of her rejection at the bottom of a crate of beer and a different blonde every other night. Always blonde, each one a punishing reminder of her betrayal, a reminder never to give my heart over to any woman to be trampled on again.

I was upfront – no strings and no promises of commitment. Just sex, plain and simple, with no emotions at risk. I made sure I always used protection – no burying the bone unless I was wearing a cock-sock. No chances of another woman telling me I'd gotten her pregnant.

That arrangement was working fine, my only priorities getting drunk and getting laid, until six months ago when Puff the One-Eyed Dragon had stopped…puffing.

Despite a reputation I know I've earned in the last year, I haven't been near a woman for the last six months of it. The only good thing I can say about having a defective dick is that it's broken the self-destructive cycle I was on. I can admit now that I fucked up. I'm not proud of my six-month knee-jerk reaction to losing Monica and the only person it damaged in the long run was me.

My best friend, Tyler, has been there for me. He knew I was licking my wounds from Monica's betrayal, but he didn't push. He just waited in the background like a good friend until I was ready to spill my guts and was there for me the night I finally did.

I'm glad things have worked out for him and his girl, Jenna. He deserves to be happy and she seems like a genuinely sweet girl. It's obvious they're madly in love and it's good to see my friend with the real deal.

But pleased as I am for them, love is for other people now. I have no need for it.

Tonight, though, a blonde bombshell has unexpectedly brought my body back to life. Something about her has unlocked a psychological block and I need to find her.

I just don't know where to start.
☐

PRUE

"We got the contract!"

Jenna and I are on our way to the game, my first football game thanks to her invitation. I've never been a football fan but Jenna's boyfriend is a line-backer for the California Cubs so she goes to almost every game.

We've only known each for a short time since Jenna moved here from Virginia to be with Tyler but we hit it off immediately, being a similar age, and we've become good friends. Jenna is also my boss at the therapy clinic where we both work, although it's weird thinking of her that way, as we get along so well.

"What contract?" I glance across at her in the passenger seat as I stop for a red light.

"For the football team!" Jenna says excitedly. "They need someone to look after the players now they're not renewing the contract with the previous company - something about them charging too much, according to Tyler. He said I should go for it and submit a care package and tender for the contract. So, I did and we got it!" It's clear to see that Jenna is buzzing.

"That's great news! Only here a month and already making

your mark. Congratulations, Boss!"

Jenna rolls her eyes at me as I pull away from the lights. "You know I hate it when you call me that," she grumbles, "but thanks, Prue. It was all done above board – no one knew about mine and Tyler's relationship. I don't want any free rides when it comes to work".

"I don't doubt that for a minute, Jen," I reassure her. "It's down to your hard work and initiative." Besides my Mom, Jenna is the most honest and moral person I've ever met. "So, what does it mean for us?"

"Well, we get to provide our whole range of therapies for the players including remedial and sports therapies. I've even got a podiatrist joining the team so we have someone on site to deal with any foot issues as well as biomechanics and orthotics. It's perfect, as the powers that be understand how beneficial it is for their players to receive those types of treatments." Jenna's voice is rich with excitement. "Now, all I need to do is get the rest of the team on board as it will mean extra hours for everyone."

"Well, I'm on board," I grin across at her, "I could use the extra money."

"I knew I could count on you, Prue. I'm scheduling a meeting next week for all the therapists so I'll have a better idea of who else is on board before deciding if I need to hire any extra staff."

"I'm sure everyone will be fine – we're a good bunch and you've made some great improvements since you started so I'm pretty sure you have us all eating out of your hand!" I grin, steering my little VW Jetta into a parking spot. "Now, let's go watch some football!"

21

"TOUCHDOWN!"

The commentator's voice announces the win and the stadium erupts. I scream, jumping up and down as I celebrate with Jenna. Who knew football could be so exciting?

"There's Tyler," Jenna points him out to me as he celebrates with his teammates on the field. "And that's his best friend, Jake, next to him."

My stomach falls into my shoes as the mountain of a player next to Tyler takes off his football helmet, revealing his dark, shaggy hair. I can't see the color of his eyes from here but there's no mistaking that chiseled face - minus the green paint.

Shrek.

Shrek, whose kiss I haven't stopped thinking about for two whole weeks.

Shrek, who is Tyler's best friend and whose real name is Jake.

I realize that Jenna is staring at me curiously as I glare at Jake, and I quickly wipe the frown from my face, turning to hug her. "That was amazing! Thank you so much for bringing me!"

Jenna chuckles at my excitement, "Anytime. It makes a nice change to have someone to sit with. I'm not sure what was more entertaining, watching you or watching the game!"

"I know, I know! I did get a little over-excited but I couldn't help it. All those manly specimens at the peak of physical fitness with butt cheeks that could crack walnuts and enormous di..."

"Okay, okay!" Jenna interrupts, holding her hands up, knowing where this conversation is headed. "It's good to know you came for the tactical strategies of the game," she laughs.

"Nah – I just came for the hot men in tight pants," I joke, fluttering my eyelashes and fanning myself dramatically with my hands.

Jenna's cell rings just as we're collecting our belongings and heading out of the stands, so I mouth that I'll meet her back at the car.

As I walk back, my thoughts return to the horrible coincidence that Shrek is none other than Tyler's friend and teammate.

I'm not one for letting any man linger in my thoughts for long, but he's managed it with one blistering hot kiss.

It's not like I haven't dated other men but there was something about his mouth on mine that seems to have left a permanent tattoo on me. He got under my defences and elicited a response that no one else ever has, one that I couldn't hide and part of the reason I turned tail and ran.

I make a quick bathroom detour before continuing to the car, fighting my way through the throngs of people exiting the stadium. When I finally get back to the parking lot I notice a Ferrari parked right up behind my little VW.

"Great," I mutter under my breath. "I've got a super-duper Ferrari so I can park wherever the hell I want!" I mimic, as if I know what the owner of the car sounds like.

I walk around and see I'm hemmed in from front and back, the Ferrari almost touching the back bumper of my VW. Marching back to my car, I unlock the door and slide behind the wheel.

I may have to perform a twenty-eight-point turn, but I should be able to drive out from the side, which is clear of cars. As I inch the car back I hear a familiar, deep voice behind me.

"What the fuck do you think you're doing?"

Oh no! Please do not let him be the owner of the Ferrari!

I turn to look behind me and my worst fears are confirmed. Jake stands there, hands on hips, his handsome face a mask of anger. I take a deep breath and turn off the engine before climbing back out of the car to face him.

"What does it look like I'm doing?" I say, matching his attitude and raising him.

"It looks like you're trying to trash my car." Jake tears his eyes away from his precious Ferrari and looks at me fully for the first time. I hold my breath waiting to see if he recognizes me. "Hasn't anyone ever told you it's illegal to reverse over other people's cars?"

I release my breath as not one spark of recognition shows in his eyes. I'm not sure why I'm so pissed about that even though I know the red-headed woman in jeans and a casual t-shirt standing before him now is a far cry from the blonde siren at the fancy dress party. "And hasn't anyone told you not to park so damn close that other people can't get out!" I retaliate, stomping to the back of my car. "I'm nowhere near your car! See? I'm a whole two inches away!" My voice drips with sarcasm.

Jake's mouth thins with anger. "Two inches too close, for my liking!"

"Then like I said, learn how to park and situations like this can be avoided."

"There'd better not be any damage," Jake snaps, inspecting

the front of the Ferrari.

The only damage will be to his face if he doesn't back the hell off! I'm not a redhead for nothing and my temper gets the better of me as I take a step closer to him. I'm tall for a woman but the top of my head barely reaches his chin. "I told you, you big, muscle-bound jackass, I was nowhere near your precious car!"

"And I told you, Carrots, if there's any damage, it'll be on your insurance!"

"Don't. Call. Me. Carrots! My name is Prudence, not Anne Fucking Shirley!" I know my complexion probably matches my hair and I can feel my body vibrating with anger. "Not that you'd remember," I can't resist adding under my breath.

"Well, whatever-the-fuck-your-name-is, look where you're going before reversing your car. You won't be so fortunate next time!" He turns on his heel, climbing into his Ferrari and driving off with a squeal of tires.

"Stupid, overbearing, arrogant. ....."

"I see you've met Jake," Jenna appears behind me, trying to keep a straight face.

"Oh, I've met him before," I reply before I can think, and Jenna looks at me with raised eyebrows. "Never mind," I mutter, climbing into the driver's seat again.

I take a deep, calming breath and fix a sunny smile on my face and Jenna obviously decides not to pursue the subject.
"Come on. Let's get you home so you can get into femme fatale mode before Tyler gets back," I waggle my eyebrows at her suggestively.

It's almost seven by the time I drop Jenna home and head back to my apartment. I'm still pissed from my run-in with Jake and the fact that he didn't recognize me, which I know is unreasonable under the circumstances.

God, what an arrogant asshat! I decide not to give him another thought as I park in my spot outside my apartment.

I live in a small gated community with a mixture of houses and apartments so there are people of all ages, including families with children and single people like myself. I really lucked out with my apartment as it's at the end of a block so my only neighbors are a lovely elderly couple.

As I lock the car, I see Mr. Grimes out front putting out the trash. "Hey, Mr. G. How's the hip?" I pluck the heavy garbage bag from him.

"Ah, thank you, Prue. What would I do without you?" he says as I dump the bag into the garbage bin. "It's been paining me a little today."

Mr. & Mrs. Grimes only moved in a few months ago but they've already become like grandparents to me. They decided to downsize after Mr. Grimes fell down the stairs at their old house and broke his hip. Our apartments are all one level so it suits them perfectly while he recovers from his hip surgery.

"Don't worry Mr. G, you'll soon be back doing everything again, including dancing with your wife," I grin.

He and his wife still make a point of going dancing together, even after more than forty years of marriage. Falling and hurting his hip has put paid to that for a while, but I'm optimistic that his dancing days aren't over just yet. "Gives me a little hope, actually,"

I smile, "knowing that there are still couples like you who are happily married after so many years. My parents divorced when I was thirteen."

"I'm sorry to hear that, dear. It must have been tough."

I shrug. "Mom and I left – we'd had all we could take with my Dad. He was into some bad stuff." I'm telling him the short version of events – very few people know the full story about why Mom and I left so suddenly. "It's all good now. Mom's in a relationship with someone else. They live upstate."

"Something tells me there's more to your story than you're saying," Mr. Grimes says intuitively, "but I'm glad to hear you and your Mom were brave enough to get out of a bad relationship. That's never an easy thing to do," he pats my hand paternally. "Where is your father now, if you don't mind me asking?"

"In jail. Where he belongs," I give him a tight smile and quickly change the subject. "Anyway, enough of me talking your ear off. Is there anything else I can help you with?"

"No, dear. You go on and enjoy your evening."

I say goodnight, checking he gets back inside okay before unlocking my front door.

My apartment is small with only the one bedroom and a small open plan kitchen, dining and living area. It's all I can afford but it's mine. I don't have a lot left over at the end of the month once I've paid my rent and utilities but I wouldn't have it any other way. There's a lot to be said for being self-sufficient and living off my own hard-earned money.

I'm kicking off my sneakers as my cell lights up with Mom's

ringtone. "Hi, Mom."

"Hey, sweet girl. How are you?"

"I'm good. You?"

"I'm good. Great, actually," Mom sounds as if she's going to burst. "Daryl asked me to marry him and I said yes!"

"Oh, Mom! That's wonderful news! Congratulations to you both! Tell Daryl he's achieved the impossible!" I chuckle.

"I'll tell him," Mom chuckles. "I never thought in a million years I'd get married again after your father."

"Well, you know what they say - true love conquers all!" I laugh.

"It certainly does, honey. Talking of," her voice takes on a teasing note, "any love life updates you want to share with your Mom?"

"Mom, seriously!" I tuck the phone under my ear as I walk to the kitchen and pour myself a glass of wine. "I am so not having this conversation with you again."

"I worry about you, Prue. It's not good to be on your own."

"I know, Mom, but it's not that simple. I'd rather be on my own than end up like you and dad." I wince as I realize how that must have sounded, "Sorry, Mom. I didn't mean it like that."

"Yes, you did, honey. And you don't need to apologize for speaking the truth, Prue."

"Anyway, it's not like I haven't tried. I've dated – even signed up to one of those online dating sites but it's just not for me." The thought of dating reminds me of my kiss with Jake. I will not think about Jake's mouth on mine. Nope, not thinking about his mouth at all. Or any other part of him.

"Prue, you are an amazing, funny, caring person and any man would be lucky to have you," Mom says. "I'm your mother so I should know. You are a beautiful woman, curves and all. Get out there and show them what they're missing. I know what happened was awful but don't let that experience stop you from living your life. If you do, he's won."

"I know you're right, Mom," I say, taking my glass of wine with me and I curling up on the sofa. "It's just that some things aren't that easy to forget."

"We both know that, honey. I only wish I'd gotten us out sooner, that it hadn't taken that man putting his hands on you to make me realize how bad things really were."

"It wasn't your fault, Mom. None of us knew what Dad had gotten himself into. You did everything you could to make it work, even when it meant sacrificing your own happiness." It always hurts me to hear Mom taking the blame for everything that happened.

"I know that now. It's hard to see the nightmare you're living in when you don't know any different," Mom sighs. "It's like lying in the sun for too long and not realizing that you've burned your skin until it's too late, only I didn't realize it wasn't just me getting burned. You were too. He was a good man before it all went to hell. I almost left it too late."

Mom pauses and I can hear her swallow back tears. "But, I've finally forgiven myself, Prue. I know now that I can't move on until I do. Daryl and I haven't known each other long, but he and I are just…right together. More so than it ever was with your father. If someone like him can love me just as I am, truly love me, then I have to believe I'm worthy of that love."

I feel a little of the weight of the past lift from my own

shoulders at hearing Mom say she's finally moving forward with her life. It's way overdue.

"I'm so happy to hear you say that, Mom. You deserve to be happy." I brush away a stray tear.

"And what about you, Prue? What about what you deserve?" Mom's voice is soft.

"I'm still figuring that out, Mom."

Letting go of the past seems to be a little harder for me.
□

JAKE

I curse as I peel out of the parking lot, my anger now directed at myself as I regret my uncharacteristic behavior. I contemplate turning around and apologising but I'm sure she's already left by now.

I'm in a foul mood. I should be happy, celebrating the fact that we've just won the most important game of the year but I couldn't wait to get out of there, hightailing it back to my car to get home. Tyler was in a hurry to get back to Jenna too, so I don't feel quite so bad that I'm not the only one to turn down after-game drinks with the guys.

I can't pinpoint it but there was something familiar about Carrots. What had she called me? Oh yeah, a muscle-bound jackass. I chuckle to myself, admiring her spunk. She probably wasn't far wrong there, judging by my shitty attitude toward her. I'm frustrated and it's showing.

It's been two weeks since the party, two weeks since I saw her and two weeks since there's been any sign of life from the womb broom. Apart from five minutes ago with Carrots. Strangely, the snake had raised its head then, which gives me hope that maybe things are getting back to normal. Not that I plan on going back to the man-ho days I wallowed in just after my break up with Monica.

It's just good to feel capable again, to feel like a man again. Maybe the damage wasn't as permanent as I'd feared if a red-headed spitfire with green eyes can...shit!

I've seen eyes that green before, looking back at me from a cab as she fled the party.

I almost crash the car as the dots connect. Carrots is *her* - my blonde bombshell. It seems my body recognized her before my eyes and brain did, which is ironic under the circumstances.

Who is she? And why is my dick particularly attracted to her? I can't believe that I've just driven away from the only woman who has given me a hard-on in the last six months. If anyone had told me a year ago that my dick would only rise for one woman I would've laughed myself silly.

What was her name? She yelled it at me when we were arguing. Anne Shirley? No, that's not right.

Prudence. Her name is Prudence.

How many women can there be with that name in California?

I intend to find out.

Tyler calls me later that evening and invites me over to his place for a post-game drink. I grab a quick shower and change into jeans and a t-shirt before heading over to his place.

Tyler answers the door to his apartment with a shit-eating grin on his face. "Hey, Jake. Come on in."

"What's got you looking so happy? Or shouldn't I ask?"

"You know. Great win. Came home to a great woman." He looks like the cat who got the cream. Seems Tyler rushed home for little post-game hide the sausage.

"Talking of, where is Jenna?" I ask.

"In the shower. She'll be out in a minute."

I follow Tyler through to the kitchen. "Thanks for the invite, Ty. I didn't really feel like getting buzzed with the boys tonight. I was kinda glad when you begged off too. At least now I'm not the only lightweight on the team," I joke.

"Hey, anything to make you look like less of a pussy," Tyler jokes, tossing me a cold bottle of beer.

We move through to the living area and I grab one of the chairs while Tyler takes a seat on the sofa just as Jenna breezes into the room. She's dressed casually in jeans and a t-shirt, her hair still wet from her shower. She plops down next to Tyler and plants a kiss on him that has me averting my eyes.

"You hear my girl landed the therapy contract for the team?" Tyler asks, proudly, putting his arm around her and pulling her against him.

"That's great news, Jenna. Congratulations." I salute her with my bottle before taking a swig.

"Thanks, Jake," Jenna curls in next to Tyler. "I have a great team of therapists, so you'll be all set." She pauses, as if remembering something. "By the way, I saw you earlier, after the game. You were going all caveman about your car."

"You saw me?"

"Yeah, you were already climbing into your car and burning rubber by the time I got there. Prue was pretty upset. You were rough on her. That's not like you, Jake," she scolds.

I ignore the last part, my heart hammering in my throat. "Prue, as in….?"

"Prue, as in my friend and work colleague. The woman you were hollering at?" Jenna says, as if explaining something to a five-year-old. "Come to think of it she said she'd met you before, but I didn't push her on it because it looked like something she didn't want to talk about. Anything you want to share?"

Prue is Jenna's friend. And her work colleague. I can't believe my fucking luck! "I'm not sure why she thinks she knows me," I say, lying through my ass with a careless shrug. "Maybe she's confusing me with someone else."

Well, well! Looks like I've found my blonde bombshell and it seems she was right under my nose all along. Now I just need to come up with a way to make this situation work to my advantage.

All the puzzle pieces are clicking into place.
☐

PRUE

The next two weeks fly by as work keeps me busier than ever. Jenna has enough therapists willing to cover the extra hours needed for the new contract, some of which involve extra time on days off and some working later into the evening. I choose the latter option, preferring to add an hour or two to an existing work day rather than having to sacrifice any of my days off.

I arrive at work one Friday, a few weeks after my run-in with Jake, ready for a busy day. I wave to Suzy on reception who single-handedly manages all the calls and appointments as well as greeting patients and taking them through to the relevant treatment rooms. The rooms are always set up for the day ahead so I'm good to go as soon as I get in.

The day flies by, as it always does when I'm busy, and before I know it I'm washing my hands and grabbing a quick glass of water before heading out to reception to collect the medical card for my last appointment of the day.

"It's a new patient," Suzy, a petite lady in her thirties with blonde curly hair, hands me the medical form. "Mr. Matthews. He's been having issues with his lower back. All the information is on the card."

"Thanks, Suzy." I take the card, giving it a quick glance as I head back to my room.

I knock lightly on the door before entering, coming to an abrupt halt as I see the man lounging casually in the chair next to the treatment couch.

"Hello, Carrots. Or should I call you Marilyn? Or maybe, by your real name, Prudence," Jake says, giving me a smug grin.

My mouth drops open in shock, unable to comprehend why Jake is here in my treatment room. "What are you doing here?" My voice comes out in an embarrassing squeak.

"This is a treatment room," Jake says calmly, "and you're a therapist. So, I think it's fairly obvious that I'm here for some... therapy."

"Really?" I'm unable to keep the hint of sarcasm from my voice as I recover from the initial shock of seeing him.

"Really," He looks me straight in the eye. "My lower back's been bothering me for a few weeks now."

Oh, I see. That's how he wants to play it. He wants a treatment? Okay, that's exactly what he'll get. Completely professional. "Right, well, if you'd like to undress down to your underwear. I'll leave the room to give you some priv..."

My words trail off and the professionalism I'm trying so hard to maintain goes out the window as Jake stands and strips off his t-shirt and sweatpants. He's already divested himself of his sneakers so he's now naked apart from his boxers and oh-my-heavenly-lord, he is one fine specimen!

I resist the urge to lick my lips as my eyes are drawn to his golden skin from the top of his broad shoulders, down his ripped abs and muscled thighs.

I'm used to seeing bodies of all shapes and sizes but the sight of a semi-naked Jake has me practically drooling on myself.

"How do you want me?" Jake asks.

Dear God, is he really asking me that question? There are so many answers I could give, none of which would be appropriate right now. "Um, face down, with your head this end," I indicate how I want him to lie. He does as I ask, dwarfing the couch with his big body.

"Where have you been feeling the discomfort?" I ask, keeping my voice matter-of-fact.

"All around here," Jake reaches 'round and touches the base of his spine, trailing his hand down to his firm right butt cheek.

I swallow hard. I can do this. No problem. "I'll need to work into your glutes. Are you okay with that?"

"Whatever you need to do to make the ache go away, Prue." His insinuation and the sound of my name on his tongue has liquid heat pouring through my veins. I'm already breathing hard and I haven't even put my hands on him yet.

In one practiced motion, I pull his boxers down below his sculpted butt cheeks, tucking a towel under the waistband to protect his underwear from the oil.

I squeeze some oil into my hands and begin to work it into his firm skin, spreading it across his back and around his buttocks. My skilled fingers and thumbs work across the smooth skin while my mind battles with my body. He's a perfect example of manhood, with his firm defined muscles, now glistening with the oil. God, I want to bend down and bite his......!

"Mmmm, that feels good, Prue. Right where your hands are now."

His moan of pleasure sets a fire in my bloodstream ending in a pool of heat between my legs. My hands linger on his skin, my fingers relishing the dips and contours as they flow up and down his back, lost in the sensation of his warm flesh.

The minutes tick by and the tension ratchets up as my fingers dance across his supple skin, the only sounds in the room that of our heavy breaths.

"Turn over, please." My voice is husky as I instruct him.

He turns onto his back and my eyes widen as I'm confronted with the impressive evidence of his arousal. My mind is telling me to be professional but my body wants other things and it's all I can do not to straddle him and rub myself against him.

My shocked eyes trail up his ripped abs and chest to his face and our eyes lock.

"Why are you doing this?" I whisper. We both know I'm not talking about the treatment. There's nothing wrong with his back - he knows it and I know it. So, what does he want?

In a quick motion, he pulls himself into a sitting position, his legs straddling the couch as he reaches out and tugs me off balance so that I land on my butt next to him.

"This is why." His breath tickles my ear, sending shivers down my neck as he takes my nerveless hands and places them over his hard erection. The feel of him there excites me, the needs of my body beginning to outweigh rational thought as my nipples harden and my breathing picks up. I've never been this sexually attracted to any man before. On the one hand, it's a relief to know that I can be attracted to a man in this way. On the other, the power it gives him terrifies me.

"Do you feel this?" Jake's mouth lingers next to my ear, his warm breath stirring the sensitised skin. "Only you can get me hard like this."

My eyes flick to his, trying to absorb what he's telling me.

"For six months, I've walked around dead from the waist down and in one second you changed all that. As soon as I put my hands on you, my body came back to life. It's why I kissed you that night at the party. I couldn't help myself." He tucks a lock of hair that's come loose from my bun behind my ear, his warm fingers lingering on my cheek.

My breathing picks up and I find myself leaning toward his touch, seeking a deeper contact with him. A part of me knows I should move away from him. I shouldn't be sitting here in the circle of his arms allowing him to touch me like this but I just can't seem make my body obey the commands of my mind.

"After you left in the cab, I went back into the party to try to find out who you were, but nobody seemed to know," Jake continues. "Then, two weeks ago, I got my ass chewed by a fiery redhead that I accused of trying to reverse over my car. I'm sorry about that, by the way. I shouldn't have taken my bad temper out on you."

I try to hide my surprise at his unexpected apology.

"There was something familiar about you and I couldn't quite pin it down until I remembered where I'd seen eyes this green before." His thumb sweeps over my cheekbone as he holds my gaze. "Then, as luck would have it, I learned that you're Jenna's friend and it wasn't difficult to find out where you worked from there."

I clear my throat. "Why are you telling me all this now? What is it you're expecting, exactly?"

"You." Jake's eyes drop to my mouth. "I want you."

I know if I lean forward an inch our mouths will meet and I can kiss him like I did that night, tangle my tongue with his as I push my hands through his hair. "So, you're proposing what?

That I sleep with you? Have sex with you because I'm the only one that can cause this?"

I'm suddenly mortified to realize that I'm still touching him there, that my fingers have been moving absently on his hard length the whole time and I pull my hands away quickly, feeling the brilliant blush that hits my cheeks.

"I'm not looking for love or commitment," Jake continues. "They're pipe dreams for other people. I got badly burned by a woman, my fiancée, just over a year ago. She told me she was pregnant with my child, but it wasn't true. The child was another man's. She'd been cheating on me."

"I'm sorry," I say, feeling an unexpected pang of sympathy for him. "That must have been rough."

"It was. I went on an almighty six-month bender and I'm not gonna lie, Prue, I drank and ... indulged in other ways. Always safe," he adds quickly. "I'm not proud of my behavior but I was hurting and I didn't know how to process the pain."

I must confess, if only to myself, that I feel a little flattered that Jake has opened up to me about his past. Pain at the betrayal of a loved one is something I can relate to, as well as the inability to process it.

"I won't sleep with you, Jake," I say firmly. "I'm not built that way. I may be physically attracted to you but that doesn't automatically mean you get to climb inside my panties."

Despite my words, the thought of him stripping me out of my underwear wreaks havoc with my body and I force myself to clamp down on the images.

I've just let slip that I'm attracted to him and for a second I consider backtracking, but what's the point? We're both adults, able to make informed and balanced decisions without our judgment being clouded by sexual desire.
Absolutely.

"I'd like to get to know you better, Prue. We've established that we're attracted to each other. Let's just see where it takes us. No promises. No pressure. Just two people enjoying each other exclusively for as long as it lasts."

My mind is telling me to run and don't look back but my body is screaming at me to take him up on his suggestion and jump his bones right here and now.

But I can't. I can't let myself get involved with him because part of me already knows that my heart won't survive the parting of ways once it's all over. And it will come to an end because Jake has already made it clear that long-term commitment isn't on the table. Even if it was, am *I* able to offer *him* that? My life isn't simple which is why I've always avoided the complications of relationships and kept men at arms-length.

"I can't, Jake. You can't just come in here and throw down a proposal like that and expect me to fall into bed with you. It doesn't work like that."

"It does if you want it to, Prue. I can feel how much your body wants mine when we're close like this. I can hear your heartbeat here," his big hand moves to cover my breast and I have to bite back a moan at the contact, "and how your breath hitches when I touch you, how your pupils dilate when you're aroused."

His fingers find my nipple as he's talking and he pinches gently, bringing forth the moan I'd tried so hard to suppress a

41

minute ago. His mouth hovers a breath from my lips and I swear I've never wanted anything more than for him to strip me bare and put his hands and mouth on me.

"What are you waiting for, Prue? True love? Prince Charming to come and sweep you off your feet? That's not real life. But this is."

His hand swallows my breast as he closes the small gap and claims my mouth. I'm helpless to resist him as his tongue slips past my lips, delving inside to fence with mine. I hear a moan and I'm not sure if it came from him or me as our mouths slide together, my hands tugging at his hair as I hold him to me, wanting more, always more.

"You see how perfectly we fit together, Prue?" Jake drags his mouth from mine and looks down to where his fingers are splayed across my breast. His thumb moves across the hard peak and I can't stop the way my breath hitches and my eyes close at the touch.

I feel his hand move away and his weight shift on the couch and it takes me a few seconds to realize that he's moved to the chair and is putting his clothes back on. When he's fully dressed, he puts a piece of paper on the end of the couch.

"My address and cell number," he says, "if you change your mind." Without another word, he turns and heads for the door.

"I won't," I whisper, as the door closes behind him.

I'm still worked up from my encounter with Jake when I get back to my apartment. I take a quick shower, imagining his hands on me as I soap my body. I run my fingers over my breasts, across my hard nipples and down between my legs, moaning at the memory of his mouth on mine.

What is it about him that affects me this way, makes me want to abandon all my defences that I've so carefully erected over the years?

My fingers find the hard, little nub of my clit, imagining that it's Jake's fingers touching me as I rub myself, feeling my orgasm build quickly as I think of his mouth and his tongue driving me insane. My release is quick and satisfying and I wonder if my body will ever truly belong to me again now that Jake has branded me with his touch.

After I've dried and dressed, I head to the kitchen to make myself a sandwich and salad. I'm just opening the fridge when my phone sings to life with Mom's ringtone.

"Hey, Mom."

"Hi, sweet girl. How was your day?"

"Busy. We've started the extra hours now so I've only been home a half hour."

"Oh, Prue, you must be exhausted. Are you sure you're not overdoing it? I wish I was a little closer so I could come and make you dinner and give you a hug." Mom's words trigger my fragile emotions and I feel tears sliding down my cheeks.

"I do too, Mom. I miss you," I sniff.

"Hey, why is my girl crying?" Mom asks softly. "What's going on, honey?"

I sink down on the sofa in the living room and tell Mom everything, from meeting Jake at the party to our argument and even about his visit to work. Mom and I have always been close and it's good to be able to share stuff like this with her.

"So, let me make sure I'm understanding this right," Mom says, matter-of-factly. "Jake kissed you at a party and you haven't been able to stop thinking about him since. Then, he went to the trouble of tracking you down to establish that the attraction is mutual before asking to see where it might take you. Am I getting this right, so far?"

"Uh, yes, but...."

"Prue, a man doesn't invest that amount of time and energy in a woman that he only wants for one night. So what if he's been around the block a few times, sexually? All the better for you because he knows what he's doing. He's obviously paid his dues in the last six months, from what you've told me. Nothing like a problem getting it up to humble a man and make him re-evaluate things."

"Mom, really?" I groan.

Mom ignores me and carries on undaunted. "Prue, honey, why are you holding back? You're twenty-three-years-old and I've been waiting and waiting for you to take the plunge, have a wild affair, live your life a little. In every possible sense of the word.

"Life is short, Prue. We both lived the nightmare with your father and if it's taught me anything, it's that you have to grab at the opportunities life gives you because they won't wait for you. It doesn't make you weak to admit that you feel something for this Jake, it makes you human. Maybe it won't be true love or happily ever after but you won't know that until you at least try. Life is about taking a few risks and regretting the things you tried, not the things you were too afraid to."

Mom's words make a lot of sense. I know I've always held a part of myself back because of what happened in the past. I don't ever want to give another man the opportunity to hurt me again or put me in a situation where I feel emotionally or

44

physically helpless, but I'm starting to understand that if I cut myself off from the pain that life might deal me, I'm also denying the potential pleasures too.

And something tells me there's a whole world of pleasure to be found in Jake's arms.

Until now, I've never met anyone worth taking a chance on - do I dare take the chance now? Or will I allow fear to keep holding me back from living a full life?

"Thanks, Mom. Talking to you always makes things seem a little clearer."

"Things are always clearer looking from the outside in, honey. I spent a lot of time learning that lesson. I'll always be here for you, no matter what happens, until I take my last breath on this earth. And then, I'll haunt you from Heaven," Mom chuckles.

"Love you, Mom."

"Love you too, Prue. To the moon and back."

As I say goodbye to Mom another sliver of the weight I've carried for so long slides from my shoulders.

Jake has cracked open the protective shell I've surrounded myself with and the thought of how he could hurt me scares me silly. But no one else has ever made me feel the way he makes me feel, like my body is truly alive for the first time. Maybe Jake will break my heart but he may also end up being the best mistake I ever make.

It's time to find out.

I'm going to pay him a visit.

JAKE

I can't settle this evening and it's the fault of the redheaded beauty who's been haunting my dreams for the last month.

I took a calculated risk going to her work today. I had to know if the attraction I feel for her is mutual and the answer was more than I could have hoped for.

She's as attracted to me as I am to her – she even said as much before withdrawing into herself again. It seems she's either running from me physically or freezing me out emotionally. My intuition tells me that there's a lot more to Prue than she allows most people to see and it makes me want to know her secrets even more.

Walking out of that room today was one of the hardest things I've ever done when all I wanted was bend her back over the treatment couch and bury my throbbing length in her. The feel of her mouth on mine and her full breast in my hand has only increased the need to get her under me, on top of me, any-which-fucking-way she likes.

I imagine how it would it feel to put my mouth on those amazing tits of hers, stroke her nipples with my tongue as I grind my needy cock against her wet pussy. I want to know if her hair there is the same fiery red as on her head.

I groan and pace to the bedroom - I need to vent some frustration and a good, hard workout is in order.

I throw on a pair of sweatpants, leaving my top half bare – I'll only sweat my way through a t-shirt so it seems pointless to put one on. I have a gym set up in the garage – nothing fancy, just some weights, a pull-up bar, a bike and a treadmill.

I warmup for ten minutes on the bike before beginning a circuit, moving from free-weights, to pull-ups, to press-ups and finishing with a sprint on the treadmill for timed intervals before starting over. I'm a big guy and I fucking hate the treadmill, but I need to work on my sprint speed so it's a necessary evil. An hour and a half later I'm dripping sweat and ready to call it quits.

I grab a quick shower and am just slipping on a pair of jeans when the door buzzer sounds. Frowning, I cross to the door, rubbing at my damp hair with a towel as I wonder who's calling this late on a Friday night.

The last person I expect to see standing on my doorstep is Prue. She looks nervous and flustered which makes me even more shocked at her next words.

"I've been thinking about our conversation earlier and I, uh, I'd like to take you up on your……."

Before she can finish, I've pulled her inside and backed her up against the closed door. The fact that she's here on my doorstep is all I need to know and I'm not taking the chance that she'll run from me again.

My intention to take things slowly has just evaporated in a puff of smoke.

I can see her chest rising and falling and I know that the sudden closeness of our bodies is affecting her just as strongly as it is me.

I lean forward so that our mouths are almost touching, my breath whispering over her lips. "No more talking, Prue. Just this." I move the extra inch and our mouths meet.

The groan that escapes her at the contact tips me over the edge and I press her roughly back against the door so that every inch of us is touching. My hips grind against her softness, my hard cock looking to ease its ache in the warm, wet place only she can provide.

I don't think she completely understands that she's given me back something I thought I'd lost, that she has all the power, and for some reason it doesn't scare me like it should.

Prue winds her arms around my neck and tangles her fingers in my hair as she holds me to her, deepening the kiss as her tongue tangles with mine in a tug of war that gives as much as it takes. I could kiss her like this and it would almost be enough, just the feel of her mouth on mine.

But I need more, more of her sweet lips on mine, her soft thighs wrapped around me and her heavy tits in my mouth.

I slide my hands down her hips and cup her ass, bringing our bodies into even closer contact so that my dick rubs against the seam of her jeans, the heat of her pussy branding me even through the thick fabric.

Grabbing the edges of her shirt, I tug it upwards and she lifts her arms to help as I peel it over her head. I break the kiss and toss the shirt on the floor, standing back a little to take in her perfectly rounded tits that almost spill from her pink lacy bra.

Her chest rises and falls as I look at her, a flush of desire coating her cheeks and making the freckles across her nose stand out. I want to kiss each and every one of those freckles, plus any others that are hiding on her body.

My need to touch her is like a compulsion as I trail my fingers from the front of her neck and down her chest to the lacy cups of her bra, slipping my thumbs under the silky material. Prue arches her back and moans as my thumbs find her hard nipples, stroking across the tight nubs until she sighs my name.

The breathy sound on her lips unleashes something inside me and my need to get her on cool sheets where I can ravish every inch of her slowly and thoroughly becomes overwhelming. I want her under me with my mouth on her soft skin and my needy cock buried balls deep in her tight hole.

I take her hand, lifting it to my lips, kissing each finger in turn before linking my hand with hers and tugging her toward the bedroom.

She stops at the doorway, seemingly hesitant to take that final step across the threshold and I feel a sudden unexpected need to reassure her.

"I won't do anything you don't want to do, Prue. I want this, more than anything I've wanted for a long time, but only if it's what you want too. You can still walk out of here now and not look back but I hope you don't because whatever this is between us, it's not just sex. Not anymore." I don't want to examine it too closely, but something shifted in me the minute I pulled her through my door and into my arms. Maybe before that.

My words seem to unlock the last of her reserve and she steps into the room, a silent signal that she's staying, that she wants this as much as I do. I release the breath I didn't realize I was holding - despite my words it would have killed me if she'd decided to leave now.

I gently lead her to the bed and sit on the end, tugging her toward me so that she's between my legs. My eyes hold her green ones as my hands go to the button of her jeans, slowly easing the zipper down and tugging them so they pool at her feet and she's stood before me in just her matching lacy briefs and bra.

I spread my hands around her hips, pulling her even closer, my thumbs stroking the sensitive skin of her soft stomach, loving the sound of her gasp as I place my lips just above the line of her panties.

Her hands go to my shoulders to steady herself as I flick my tongue across her skin to taste her, my thumbs continuing their torturous circles, moving closer and closer to the heat between her legs.

"Jake!" She moans my name.

"What is it you want, Prue? Do you want my mouth on you here?" I kiss the soft skin of her stomach above her panties, "Or my hands here?" I sweep my hands around her hips to squeeze her juicy ass as my mouth hovers next to her lace covered mound.

Prue's hands thread through my hair and she answers me by pulling my head to her heat, her body moving restlessly with the need for my mouth on her.

I hook my thumbs into the sides of her panties and slide them down her legs so she can step out of them. "I'm going to put my mouth on you now, Prue," I whisper. "I'm going to open you up to my lips and my tongue until you scream my name and cum in my mouth."

My words elicit another moan and the sound has my cock straining against the confines of my jeans. I languish in the feeling of not only being capable, but also of being the most potent I've ever been. And all because of this redheaded beauty in front of me.

I want to pleasure her in a way that she'll never forget, a way that she deserves, because her pleasure is just as important, if not more so, than my own. I've never been a selfish lover, but with Prue it feels different, more intense and I won't stop until I've wrung every drop of ecstasy from her beautiful body.

I nibble my way down her stomach, grazing the silky skin with my teeth as my hands smooth around her ass cheeks, circling inwards until my thumbs reach her hot slit and gently spread her folds apart. She's already wet for me, her juices shining against the dark auburn curls of her pussy and I can't hold back any longer as the need to taste her becomes overwhelming.

Prue jerks as my mouth settles over her and the tip of my tongue finds her hard, little nub. Her moans become louder as my hands grip her hips, adjusting her so that I can give her the pressure she needs and she grinds herself against my mouth until I'm buried nose deep in her wetness.

Keeping hold of one of her hips, I slide the middle finger of my other hand inside her tight hole, working it gently in and out, fucking her with my finger as I suck on her clit. I can feel the tremors of her approaching orgasm as her tight pussy grips my finger and her hands clench in my hair.

Suddenly she throws back her head and shouts my name as she cums, the contractions pulsing against my hand and mouth as her body quivers with her release.

Despite the steely hardness of my still aching cock, a warm feeling unfurls in my chest at the pleasure I've just given her and the feeling expands as she catches her breath and looks down at me, smiling shyly.

"Oh, wow! That was...um...I'm sorry, I think I may have gotten a little loud for a minute there." The blush of embarrassment staining her cheeks makes her words even more endearing.

51

"Be as loud as you want, sweetheart," I growl. "Scream the fucking place down for all I care. The sound of your orgasm is the hottest thing I've ever heard and I want to hear it again."

I fall backward onto the bed, bringing her with me so that she's straddling my hips. She's wearing the pink lacy bra and nothing else and she looks like a dream come true with her fiery hair tangling around her flushed cheeks. The sight of her on top of me like this takes my breath away.

"What about you?" Prue asks, her eyes dropping to the very obvious hard-on that my jeans do nothing to disguise.

"Don't worry about me, sweetheart. I've waited this long – I can wait a little longer." The smile she gives me transforms her face from beautiful to stunning. "In the meantime, you look a little hot. Let me help you out of this."

My hands go to the clasp of her bra, releasing it and watching spellbound as her tits spill from the lacy material. Instinctively, her hands go to cover her bareness, but I capture her wrists, stilling her movements. "Don't hide yourself from me, Prue. Your body is beautiful, every curve, every valley, and I won't be happy until I've tasted every fucking inch of you."

I reach up and fill my hands with her magnificent tits, thumbing her nipples and watching as she throws her head back, moaning my name. "Do you like it when I do this, Prue? When I stroke your nipples? Lean down towards me, I want those perfect tits in my mouth, so I can taste those nipples with my tongue."

She does as I ask, leaning her body over me so that her tits are within reach of me. I push them together, lifting my head so that I can tongue both rosy little nubs more easily, using my mouth and teeth on her until she's panting and squirming above me.

52

Having her like this, her beauty spread naked on my body, hearing her little moans and gasps, makes me feel like a fucking God. "Tell me what you want, sweetheart. Tell me and it's yours."

Prue sits back and settles her weight over the top of my thighs, reaching for the fastening of my jeans. "I want all of you."

PRUE

I almost blush at the boldness of my demands but I'm beyond rational thought as I work buttons out of holes.

Jake lifts his hips so that I can slide his jeans down his muscular legs, kicking them off the end of the bed.

My hands smooth up his calves and thighs until I reach his impressive erection, cupping him gently and then more firmly as Jake lifts his hips with a moan. I never realised how erotic it would be to hear the sounds of his pleasure - pleasure I'm giving him.

I slide my fingers under the waistband of his boxers and Jake lifts his hips again so that I can pull them slowly down. His hard shaft springs free, angling up and away from his body.

My eyes widen as I take in the full length and girth of him and a niggle of worry blooms in my stomach at the thought that I may not be able to fit all of him.

I push the niggle away as I circle him with my hands, smoothing my fingers down the velvet steel of his manhood. I watch, fascinated, as a little clear liquid leaks from the end and it seems the most natural thing in the world to lean down and lick it away with my tongue.

Jake jerks and moans at the touch of my mouth and I feel a surge of womanly power at his reaction to me. I lick and suck him, finding sensitive spots as I go and sipping the salty liquid that reappears before taking as much of his length into my mouth as I can.

"Oh God, Prue! That feels so fucking good!" Jake growls, his hands cupping the back of my head and tangling in my curls as he holds me to him.

I release his swollen shaft from my mouth with a pop and work my way up his body, nibbling and licking over the ridges of his abs and chest, pausing at his flat, male nipples to lavish some attention there.

"You're driving me crazy, sweetheart," Jake groans. "I can't hold on much longer!"

"Then don't," I reply, wanting nothing more in this moment than the feel of him inside my body, filling me up and making me whole. I want to give him the same pleasure he just gave me

Jake reaches across to the bedside cabinet and takes out a condom, looking at it closely. "Just checking they're still in date. It's been so long and I really wasn't expecting you to change your mind," he says with a wry smile.

His honesty is touching and the knowledge that I'm his first woman for some time, the only woman that's been able to arouse him like this, melts away the last of my reservations.

He must see these thought processes playing out across my face because he reaches up, stroking my cheek with his fingers. "Things are different now, Prue. I'm not the person I was six months ago and I'm glad that I get to share this experience with you - and only you. God, I'm so fucking nervous it feels like my first time all over again!"

"You are?" I say, shocked. "But, you seem so confident, so sure of yourself."

"Looks can be deceiving, sweetheart," he says and my body warms at the endearment. "With you this feels…different."

His words make my heart swell with hope and I take the packet from his fingers, tearing it open and removing the condom. My fingers tremble as I try to sheath his long length and his hands cover mine, guiding me until it's in place.

Jake lies back against the pillows. "This is your show, Prue - I'm all yours."

I swallow nervously. It's almost as if he knows that it's important for me to be in control.

I straddle him so that his shaft is pressing against my opening and reach between us to hold him, rubbing the head of him against me, coating him in my juices so that it's easier for me to take the first inch of him into me.

"God, you feel amazing, Prue. You're so tight!" Jake groans his pleasure under me as I press down another inch, waiting for my body to open up further before pressing down again.

I bite the inside of my lip through the burn of the pain as I lift off his length slightly and bear down again, my eyes drawn to where our bodies are joined as I watch him going into me. I repeat the process again and again until he's buried so deeply in me it feels like he's touching my womb.

I sigh as the burning pain eases and look up, realising that Jake has been watching me the whole time, his eyes alive with a pleasure that takes my breath away.

I begin to undulate my hips up and down, my tight channel gripping his engorged shaft as I rise and sink on him. All the while our gazes are locked on each other, making our physical connection even more poignant.

My movements become faster as Jake grips my hips, his thrusts matching mine as our bodies meet in the middle, the sounds of our sex loud in the quiet room. All control is gone as his body pumps into mine faster, harder, deeper, and I grip him, hold him to me in the most elemental way there is.

"Shit! Prue, I'm sorry! I can't hold on any longer. I'm gonna cum!" Jake's voice is ragged with passion and I watch in fascination as his face contorts with his orgasm. "Oh God, Prue!"

He throws his head back and shouts his release as the convulsions of his body seem to go on endlessly, his hands gripping my hips almost painfully as he grinds me to him and I feel the warmth of his seed flowing into me even through the protection of the condom.

It takes a while for him to catch his breath and come down from his high but when he does, his eyes fly open, pinning me with his accusing gaze.

"Why didn't you tell me you were a virgin?"

My eyes close briefly, realizing I've been rumbled. "I was hoping you wouldn't be able to tell," I whisper. Suddenly it's all too much and to my embarrassment, I feel tears spill down my cheeks.

"Hey, hey," Jake pulls me into his arms, tucking by body into his as he rolls us onto our sides, our bodies still intimately joined. "It's okay, baby. It's okay."

Unknowingly, he whispers the same words my Mom said to me years ago, unlocking a torrent of emotion that I've kept buried since then. It's been so long since I've really cried. I've denied myself the release of tears because I'm scared that once I start I'll never stop, that my emotions will continue to spill out of me like lava from a volcano.

"Shhh. Don't cry, sweetheart," Jake's soft words of comfort wash over me as he strokes my back, feathering kisses along my brow, my cheeks and my eyes. His tenderness is unexpected and despite the force of my emotions, there's a sense of peace to be found in the circle of his arms, a safety that I've never felt before.

Eventually my tears slow, leaving my eyes puffy and I know I must look a mess. "I'm sorry. I didn't mean to cry all over you."

"You don't have to apologise, Prue." Jakes tips my head back, his thumb moving gently back and forth along my jawline as he captures my gaze with his. "God, I thought I'd hurt you when you started to cry! If I'd known it was your first time I would have taken more time, been gentler with you. Why didn't you tell me?"

"Because I didn't want to take the chance that you'd change your mind if you knew," I admit. "It took all my courage to come here, Jake, and I'd made up my mind I wanted my first time to be with you."

Jake closes his eyes briefly, as if in pain. "You give me too much credit, Prue, to think I would've been that noble, but the truth is I wanted you too much to send you away. Why did you change your mind?"

"Would you believe it if I told you it was because of my Mom?"

Jake raises his eyebrows in surprise. "Your Mom told you to come have sex with me?"

I laugh at his expression as I think about that for a second. "I guess she kind of did - although she didn't put it quite that bluntly. I spoke with her on the phone and she just reminded me that life is all about having the courage to reach out for what you want. I haven't wanted anyone enough to do that - until now." I'm taking a chance admitting that to him but I've just shared my body with this man, so trusting him with a little of my inner emotions seems only right.

"Your Mom sounds like an amazing woman. I must remember to thank her when I meet her."

My heart skips a beat, wondering if Jake realizes what he's just said. Maybe his attraction to me is more than just physical if he's talking about meeting Mom.

"She's amazing." I feel like my words don't even come close to expressing how awesome she is. "We've been through so much together."

Jake frowns. "That sounds serious."

I shrug one shoulder and reach up to smooth his dark hair back from his brow. He captures my hand and brings it to his lips, nibbling on my fingers. "We had it tough when I was growing up. It was just me and her and she had to make a lot of sacrifices to keep a roof over our heads and food in our stomachs." I can't tell him the full horror of our past. He'd most likely run a mile if he knew the secrets Mom and I have had to keep.

He leans forward, kissing me slowly with breathless tenderness, his lips lingering against mine. "Thank you." He sees my questioning look. "For sharing a part of yourself with me. For choosing me to be your first."

I blush. "I'm not sorry. I'm glad it was you."

"I'm sorry I couldn't hold off long enough for you to cum again," Jake's frankness makes me blush. "It's been so long and I was too far gone - you drove me crazy with that mouth of yours."

59

"It was amazing, watching you. It's one of the most erotic things I've ever seen. I didn't know it could feel like that." Despite my shyness, I'm still amazed how comfortable it is being like this with Jake, having such an intimate conversation.

"I promise I'll make it up to you later, over and over and over..." he kisses me softly, "...but right now, I'm going to run us a bath." He leaps from the bed in one fluid motion.

"Run us a bath?"

"It'll help with any...parts of you that are sore," he says, arching his eyebrows and I can't help but laugh as he disappears into the bathroom, completely at ease with his own nudity.

I snuggle down into the bed as I hear running water, feeling warm inside and out, hardly able to believe all that has happened in the last few hours.

"Woman, get your sexy ass in here!" Jake hollers from the bathroom a few minutes later.

I smile and gather up the bed sheet and wrap it around me as I follow the sound of his voice. I come to a halt at the bathroom door as I see Jake is already immersed in the foamy water.

"You won't be needing that," he says, motioning to the sheet.

I take a deep breath and untuck the sheet, letting it drop to the floor and standing before him in all my naked glory - such as it is. I resist the urge to cover myself as his hot gaze roams my whole body, lingering on my full breasts and rounded hips and thighs.

"Beautiful," he whispers, and the heat of his gaze causes my nipples to harden and a fire to ignite between my legs. "Come here and let me show you how beautiful you are, Prue, because I don't think you realize it."

I step into the tub and turn so that my back is to him as I slide into the hot water. I can't help a groan as the heat envelops me, relaxing muscles that I hadn't realised were tight.

Jake pulls me back against him, his hands spreading across my stomach as he positions us so that he's spooning me from behind and I gasp when I feel that he's already more than capable again.

Grabbing a cloth from the side of the bath he dips it in the water and starts to gently wash me, his arms encircling me from behind and I just enjoy the feeling of his hands on me this way. I arch slightly as he rubs the cloth over my breasts and around my nipples, then moves to my arms and upper back, sweeping my hair to one side.

"What's this?" Jake pauses in his ministrations, gently touching the scars where my neck meets my shoulder. "Looks like someone tried to take a bite out of you," he chuckles as he bends to kiss the scar.

In another time and place, the caress would be endearing. But not now. He has no idea how close to home he is or the locked box of dark memories that his words threaten to unleash. I swallow hard, trying to compose myself and calm the panic that has suddenly sprung to life and almost overwhelms me.

"I don't even remember how that happened. Probably some silly thing I did as a kid." My laugh sounds false to my ears.

I've never had to lie about the scar before because no one else has ever gotten close enough to see it. I've always made sure it's covered with my clothing or my hair and I've refused to look at it for so long that I almost had myself convinced it wasn't there anymore.

The past is rearing its ugly head and I need to keep the nightmares at bay.

The water sloshes around us as I turn my body to face Jake, a sudden desperate need overtaking me.

"Please make love to me, Jake. I need you inside me. Right now."

JAKE

I'm momentarily taken aback by the emotion in Prue's eyes and the desperate edge to her voice. Something's not adding up here and I intend to find out what but for now, I'm more than happy to give her what she needs.

We hardly spare the time to dry off before our mouths collide, our breathing ragged as our burning desire for each other outweighs the need to be soft and slow.

Without breaking our kiss, I lift her and she wraps her legs around my waist as I carry her back through to the bedroom, lowering her to the bed. I go to move back a little so she can scoot further onto the bed, but she clings to me, holding me to her as if she's afraid to let me go.

"Don't stop touching me, Jake," she moans, "not even for a second. Please!"

"Don't worry, sweetheart, I'm not going anywhere," I promise, and a part of me already knows that I mean to follow through on that promise on some deeper level. In a short space of time, this woman has unleashed protective instincts in me that I've never felt before, not even with Monica.

Prue pulls me with her as she lies back, my weight settling

against her and pressing her into the mattress, our bodies fitting together like two pieces of a puzzle. Her hands trail down my back to my butt and she grabs my ass, spreading her legs below me and opening herself up to my throbbing cock, bringing me into stark contact with her moist opening.

"Don't make me wait, Jake, please!"

Her plea shatters my self-control and without thinking I grab her hips and bury myself in her in one smooth thrust, all thought of protection gone as I sink into her hot, wet depths. Prue arches up off the bed towards me as I impale her and her eyes snap open as she also realises we're going bareback.

"Give me two seconds, sweetheart." I force myself to pull out of her long enough to sheath myself with a condom. Shit, that was a close call. Strangely, though, the thought of our baby growing in her belly doesn't freak me out like it should. Like it would have even a few hours ago.

I sit back on the bed and pull Prue on top of me so that she's straddling me, her long legs tucked underneath her next to my hips. She immediately sinks down on the full length of my cock, making us both moan as her tight pussy takes me balls deep.

Prue rides me like a woman possessed and it's all I can do not to shoot my load within the first few seconds of her hips rising and falling against me. I reach up and cup her tits, thumbing her nipples and making her cry out as she increases her pace.

In one smooth motion, I tip her backward so that I'm on top of her with her legs over my shoulders. "I'm gonna go deep now, sweetheart. So fucking deep!"

Her eyes widen as I thrust down into her, the angle of our bodies making it possible for me to plunge into her so fully that her eyes roll back and I feel I like my cock is going to detonate.

I reach between us and slip my thumb between her slick folds and strum her clit while I pump in and out of her body. Within seconds, the friction causes her to shoot over the edge, her legs tightening around me as she grinds her pussy against my thumb and my cock and screams my name.

Seeing and hearing her convulse and feeling her warm juices on my cock is enough to trigger my own orgasm. With one last thrust I shoot an endless stream of cum into her as my whole body spasms against her and I experience the hardest, hottest climax of my entire life.

When my breathing has steadied and my legs can support my weight again, I tear myself away from her and go clean myself up as quickly as I can, not wanting to be separated from her for one second longer than I have to.

Prue is almost asleep, completely sated from our lovemaking, as I climb back into bed and pull her into my arms. She curls her body around mine trustingly, tucking her chin into my neck and pressing a kiss to my throat as she murmurs sleepily.

My chest feels tight with emotion as hold her to me. I'm never going to be able to get enough of this feeling, of this woman, and the realization floors me. I thought I'd be able to get her out of my system once we'd had sex but if anything, I want her more now than ever and that scares the shit out of me. What had I said to her earlier?

Just two people enjoying each other exclusively for as long as it lasts.

Well, I hope she's prepared for it to last because there's no way I can let her go now, not after what we've shared together tonight.

I know there are parts of herself that she's keeping hidden, secrets she's not ready to share. Something happened to her in the past and her reaction to my question about the scar on her neck has my instincts on red alert.

I want her to know that she can share those secrets with me, but something tells me I'm going to have to tread carefully.

She's mine now and I won't do anything to jeopardise that.

PRUE

Most of Saturday passes in a blur. It's as if Jake has unleashed my inner sex monster and I can't get enough of him. It seems to be mutual because Jake is equally unable to keep his hands off me.

It feels like we're always finding some way to touch each other, whether it be a soft kiss, a twining of fingers, or having him buried deeply within me, wringing every last drop of pleasure from my body in an orgasm that makes me scream his name.

The loud gurgling of my stomach immediately after makes us laugh and reminds us that we haven't eaten for almost a day.

"Come on, woman. Get dressed and I'll make us something to eat." Jake pulls me to my feet, giving my bare butt a little smack as I head toward the bedroom on legs that feel boneless with pleasure.

I dress quickly in my clothes from the night before, which takes longer than usual as they seem to be scattered at various points throughout the bedroom. My t-shirt is by the front door and the memory of how it got there puts a flush on my cheeks.

Once I'm dressed I take a look around. I know that Jake's apartment is on the third floor of a complex but apart from the bedroom and bathroom, I have no recollection of what the rest of his apartment looks like.

The living, dining and kitchen area is open plan like my own apartment, only Jake's is much bigger and he has a guest bedroom.

The space is simply, yet tastefully, decorated although it lacks a woman's influence, something that I find reassuring as the thought of another woman in here putting little touches on the place unleashes a little green-eyed monster in my chest.

A delicious smell causes my stomach to gurgle again and I see Jake moving around the kitchen looking completely at home.

"Come and eat." He places a plate overflowing with freshly baked biscuits on the dining table where he's already put out cutlery, jelly and butter.

Jake sits and I move to take a seat on the opposite side of the table, only to be stopped short and hauled onto his lap.

"That's too far away," he growls and the possessiveness of his words seeps straight into my heart.

"I'll squash you," I try to object but it's half-hearted as I love being this close to him.

"Sweetheart, I'm six five and weigh two forty - I don't think there's any danger of you squashing me." His arms circle me as he reaches forward for a biscuit and passes it to me.

I slather it with butter before taking a huge bite, moaning as it hits my taste buds. "Mmmm, this is so good! You're spoiling me. Complete sex god *and* you can cook."

"Hey, I'm multi-talented," he grins, pulling my head down for a kiss and licking a spot of butter from the corner of my mouth.

"And modest!" I say, smiling against his lips.

"Not where you're concerned. I really do feel like a sex god after last night. And this morning. Oh, and let's not forget an hour ago." I punch his arm lightly, blushing. "And there's that beautiful blush that I love," he teases. "I just cannot comprehend how you were still a virgin, why someone didn't snap you up before. Weren't you ever tempted?"

I shrug one shoulder. "I dated. I even joined an online dating agency for a while but it was a disaster."

"What happened?" Jake asks curiously.

"Well, I only went on two dates. The first guy totally lied about his age. He said he was twenty-five but turned out he was in his sixties."

I glare at Jake who's trying to keep a straight face. "The second guy seemed okay at first, but then during dinner he felt it was important to tell me that he could only get turned on by being tickled with feathers and that his penis was shaped like a banana."

69

Jake throws back his head and roars with laughter. He stops when I feign a hurt look and pulls me to him for a hug. "I'm sorry. What did you do?" he says, still trying to smother his laughter.

"I told him I was allergic to feathers and banana shaped penises and I left. Quickly."

His chest rumbles underneath me as laughs again. "You're precious, Prue."

"You're not so bad yourself." I kiss him gently, teasing his lips with mine. "Apart from, you haven't fed me coffee. I need at least five cups to avoid the ugliness that is caffeine-withdrawal and believe me, it won't be pretty!"

"I'm all out but your wish is my command. I'll run to the store and get you the finest freeze-dried coffee they have."

"My hero!" I sigh, placing my hands over my heart and batting my lashes.

"But, I need one of these to tide me over while I'm gone," Jake says, spearing his fingers through my hair and kissing me so thoroughly that I'm breathless by the time he pulls away, my mouth automatically following his for more. "We'll finish this when I get back," he breathes. "I won't be long."

He puts me back on my feet before standing and collecting his keys from the kitchen worktop.

When he's gone, I clear away the breakfast things and head back into the bedroom. I remake the bed although I'm not sure if I'm staying here tonight or if Jake even wants me to. Part of me wants to stay and part of me is scared to. I think I may already be in over my head.

I'm just plumping the pillows when the door buzzer sounds. It can't be Jake as he'd let himself in so I consider ignoring it but whoever it is they're persistent, and the buzzer goes again.

I walk to the door and look through the peephole to see a stunning blonde in a short skirt which shows off her impossibly long, tanned legs.

I open the door. "Hi, can I help you?"

"Who are you?" Blondie asks rudely, pushing past me into the apartment.

"I'm Prue. Is there something I can help you with?" I say, trying to hold on to my temper with the woman's high-handed attitude.

"I came to see Jakey," Blondie says, strolling around the apartment as if she owns it.

Jakey? Seriously? "I'm sorry but he's not here right now but I'll tell him you called…?" I leave the question hanging.

"Kaylee. I'm on the cheer squad." Ah, the scrap of material that passes for a skirt becomes clear now. "I don't mind waiting, Pris."

I count to ten before answering. "It's Prue. And you may not mind waiting but I *do*, so if you'd like to give me a message I'll be happy to pass it along to *Jakey* when he gets back."

71

Kaylee turns to face me, giving me her full attention for the first time since she breezed through the door. She looks me up and down and immediately dismisses me as any source of competition. "This isn't your apartment so it's really not your decision to make."

I smile. "You're right, it isn't my apartment. But the man who owns it definitely is - in every way that matters."

Instead of getting angry as I expected, Kaylee tosses back her long blonde hair and laughs. "Really? The idea of Jakey belonging to one woman is ridiculous!" There's a bitter edge to her voice. "Oh, didn't he tell you that he and I have a thing going?" She pouts and adopts an innocent expression. "Then let me enlighten you." The innocent look drops from her face. "He's mine."

I don't reply straight away, narrowing my eyes at her as I take in her skimpy outfit, carefully teased curls and immaculate makeup. I'm good with body language so I also notice her overconfident stance and the nervous little tick at the corner of her mouth.

"Tell me, how long did you wait to come up here after you saw Jake leave?" I ask.

Kaylee's mouth drops open at my question. "I have no idea what you're talk..."

"Oh, I think you do," I interrupt. "I think you wanted to come up here and see just who Jake has in his apartment. What happened? Did he turn you down?" I watch with a glimmer of satisfaction as Kaylee's face turns red with anger. "If you're here to warn me off, you're too late. And as for Jake being yours?" I pause, looking her straight in the eye. "Where I'm from, possession is nine tenths of the law, so I'm pretty sure that only leaves one tenth up for grabs. Oh no, wait! I had that last ten inside me last night. And this morning. Oh, and this afternoon about an hour before you arrived."

I smile sweetly at her, holding the door open for her as she storms back through it, tears glistening in her eyes.

"Bitch!" She throws the insult at me as she stomps out.

"Yes, you are." I slam the door as soon as she crosses the threshold, turning to lean back against it as I release a shaky breath.

Wow! That was......disturbing.

Despite her actions, a tiny part of me feels a little sorry for Kaylee, especially seeing her holding back tears as she left.

Only a very insecure woman would deliberately come here like that to try and cause trouble. Of course, I'd totally bluffed the seriousness of my relationship with Jake, but damned if I was going to let Blondie know that!

When Jake walks through the door twenty minutes later I'm curled up on the sofa, thumbing through the issue of *Sports Illustrated* that was lying on the coffee table.

"Sorry I took so long, I decided only the best would do for my woman, so I went all the way to Columbia for freshly ground beans," he laughs, and I raise my eyebrows at him. "Okay, okay. Maybe not Columbia but they were out of freeze dried at the local store so I had to go to the next one over."

"You had a visitor while you were gone," I keep my voice neutral.

73

"A visitor?" Jake raises his eyebrows in question.

"Beautiful blonde by the name of Kaylee." I see the recognition on Jake's face and try not to let the hurt show. Despite my assumed confidence while Kaylee was here, her appearance has raised a few insecurities of my own.

"What the hell did she want?" All the soft teasing from a minute ago has left Jake's voice.

"She came to warn me off you, to tell me that you two have a thing going and that you belong to her." I'm amazed how calm my voice sounds when my stomach is doing loops.

"Fuck!" Jake runs a hand roughly through his hair. "Prue, she's lying! The woman is nothing but trouble. I don't know what her issue is but she's been chasing after every guy on the team. She hit on me a few months ago and I told her I wasn't interested but it seems she didn't believe me. I swear to God I there is nothing going on between us!" Jake looks like he's about to explode.

I stand up from the sofa and walk toward him, stopping just in front of him and holding his gaze. "I know, Jake. I believe you."

"You do?"

"You were upfront with me about your past from the start. I accepted your past before I came to your door last night. Plus, I'm good at reading people and she was lying through her ass."

Jake closes his eyes and lets out a sigh. "I'm the first to admit that I...went off the tracks for a while after Monica but I was faithful to her the whole time we were together - she was my first so I guess I took her rejection all the harder because of that."

My eyes widen as I absorb what he's telling me. "She was your first?"

"Yeah….and almost my last after what happened." Jake sits on the sofa and I move to sit next to him, waiting for him to continue.

"I walked in on her and her lover in our bed and as I was throwing them out Monica screamed at me that I'd never been enough for her, in or out of bed." My heart breaks for him that another woman would treat him so shoddily.

"It devastated me. Like I said, I was a man-ho there for a while after we split. I'm not proud of it now, it's not who I really am, but I was hurting at the time. Eventually, it all caught up with me and I ended up with my…. uh…. little problem." A ruddy color stains his cheeks and I realize he's embarrassed.

"Hey, less of the 'little'," I grin, trying to lighten the mood as I move to straddle him, threading my hands through his hair and tipping his head back so that he's looking at me. "She must have been mad to say those things to you, because last night was the most amazing experience of my life." I lean forward and kiss him softly.

"It's safe to say that from the moment I met you at the party, I've been a walking hard-on," he breathes against my mouth. "I know I said yesterday that we should just enjoy this while it lasts, but everything's changed since then, since last night. For me, at least."

"For me, too," I whisper, my heart fluttering in my chest at his words.

I'm in love with this man and I'm pretty sure I have been since I first laid eyes on him. It's the only thing that would have brought me here last night. Our physical attraction is beyond anything I could have imagined but I know that alone wouldn't have been enough for me.

Some part of me knew last night that I had already fallen for him, but being here with him, spending time together, making love with him, has brought my feelings into sharp focus. I know that Jake hasn't made any declarations of love to me, but I can see that things have shifted for him emotionally and that's a start. I can wait for more. I can wait for him.

I shift my position, pressing my body against him and his arms come around me, holding me so tightly that I almost lose my breath.

"I'm sorry you had to deal with Kaylee," Jake sighs, tangling his hands in my hair.

"It's okay. People and things from the past only have the power to hurt us if we let them." I wish I could truly believe my own words but it seems like the right thing to say to alleviate Jake's guilt.

"And what about your past, Prue? What about the hurt that you don't talk about?"

His insight shocks me and I'm struggling for some way to answer that question when the sound of my cell phone interrupts us.

Climbing from Jake's lap, I go to retrieve it from my purse by the front door. "Hey, Mom."

"Prue? I've been calling you! Why didn't you answer your phone?"

"Sorry, Mom, I haven't had chance to check my phone. I've been.... busy. What's up? You sound upset."

"Oh God, Prue, he's out! He got out over a week ago!"

My stomach falls to the floor as I try to comprehend Mom's words.

The man who tried to rape me, the one we put behind bars almost ten years ago, is a free man.

JAKE

The color drains from Prue's face as she listens to her Mom on the other end of the phone and concern has me up and out of my seat toward her.

"Mom, I'll call you back in a little bit okay? I'm not home right now, so give me a half hour. And don't worry."

"What's up?" I ask, as Prue ends the call and turns to me. "Everything okay?"

"Yeah, yeah." Prue answers distractedly, all traces of the contented woman of a few minutes ago gone. "Listen, I'm really sorry, but I need to go."

"Go where? What's going on Prue?" I try not to let the frustration I'm feeling show in my voice.

Prue sighs, "It's my Mom. She's upset, something about a huge argument with her fiancé. I need to talk to her, calm her down and find out what's going on and it's better if I do that at my place. I would've had to head back there sometime today anyway."

Prue's sudden strange behavior makes me feel that she's not telling me the whole truth about whatever is going on with her Mom. I don't want to her to go but I can't very well keep her here. "I'll come with you."

"No, no, it's fine, thank you. It's better if I go on my own and speak to Mom and then I'll come back later. I mean, if you want me to?" She looks at me uncertainly.

"Oh, I want you back here, Prue," I say firmly and pull her toward me, wrapping my arms around her. "You've got my number?" Prue nods. "Call me if you need me, okay?"

"I will. I shouldn't be too long. I'll talk to Mom and grab some clean clothes and I'll be back." She reaches up and pulls my head down to hers and kisses me, her mouth lingering on mine.

It almost feels like she's kissing me goodbye.

I pace the floor once Prue has left, unable to settle. Things are not adding up and every sense I have is telling me that Prue is keeping secrets. Part of me is pissed that she doesn't feel she can share them with me but another part reminds me that I didn't exactly promise her happily ever after when we started this thing, so why would she? I tried to tell her earlier, but I'm not sure that she understands how much my feelings have changed, that I'm in this for the long-haul now.

I want to know when she's hurting, make her laugh when she's feeling low and hold her in my arms while we make love. And I want her to do the same for me.

Before I can think about it, I'm grabbing my keys and heading out the door.

Tyler looks surprised to find me standing on his doorstep late on a Saturday afternoon. He takes one look at my face and opens the door wide to let me in.

I go straight through to the living area, taking a seat in the chair while Tyler sits on the sofa.

"What's up?" Ty doesn't waste any time with pleasantries.

"I need an address for Prue."

Tyler looks confused for a minute. "Jenna's friend? "Why?"

I tell Ty the whole story, from my first encounter with Prue at the party up to her odd phone call with her Mom.

When I'm done, Ty leans back on the sofa, crossing one ankle over his knee. If he's shocked or surprised, he doesn't show it.

"So, you want Prue's address so that you can go and check she's okay?"

"Yeah. When she left, she seemed really shaken up. I know she said her Mom needed to talk but I think there's more to it than that."

"You've got feelings for her," Ty makes it a statement rather than a question.

I just nod and Tyler lets out a breath. "Ah, man! You've got it bad. Welcome to the club."

He pulls out his phone and taps in a number. "Hey, baby. Listen, I need Prue's address. I'll explain later." Ty grabs a pen and notepad from the side table and scribbles down an address. "Great, thanks baby. Hurry home. Yeah, love you too."

Ty ends the call and holds the piece of paper out to me. "Don't fuck it up, Jake."

It's dark by the time I pull up outside Prue's apartment. I don't see Prue's VW anywhere, so I get out and head up the path to her front door, ringing the doorbell. Seconds tick by and there's no answer so I ring again.

I'm just debating what to do next when an elderly gentleman pokes his head out from the apartment next door.

"Are you looking for Prue?"

"Yeah, I thought she was home," I reply, wondering where she could be.

"Lots of people looking for Prue tonight. There was another guy here earlier looking for her. You a friend?" The elderly guy looks me up and down and I hold back a chuckle when I realize I'm being sized up. The old guy obviously likes to look out for Prue.

"Yeah, something like that."

"Well, another chap came by earlier and they left. Saw them on the way out and they mentioned The Java Spot. It's a coffee shop just 'round the corner. You'll be able to catch them there."

I thank the old guy and climb back into the car. My mind is all over the place as I digest what I've just been told.

Prue told me she was coming back here to talk with her Mom, grab a few clothes and head back to my place. So why the fuck is she out having coffee with another man?

I clench my hands on the steering wheel until my knuckles turn white and my fingers are numb. There's a logical explanation. I'll just head on over to the coffee shop and everything will be fine.

It takes less than five minutes for me to find The Java Spot and as I pull into the parking lot I see Prue's little VW parked at the end.

I drive the Ferrari forward slowly and as I do, my headlights pick out two people in the back. Two people making out. Definitely a man, although I can't see his face behind a mane of fiery red hair as they kiss passionately.

82

I process all this in the few seconds it takes me to drive past the car and out the exit on the other side of the parking lot. I don't stop until I'm back at my apartment.

I let myself in and head straight for the drinks cabinet, pouring myself a neat whiskey.

My mind can't process what I've just seen. My Prue kissing another man in the back of her car! And not just kissing, but making out passionately.

History is repeating itself, only this time the pain is unbearable. I know now that what I felt at Monica's betrayal was nothing more than bruised pride and a dented ego. The hurt I felt then is nothing compared to the gut-wrenching pain that I feel now. I'd promised myself never again, locked my heart up and kept it safe from harm until I fell for a redheaded fire-cracker who I'd thought was as beautiful inside as she was out. What a fucking stupid fool!

Getting burned once is bad enough, but twice?

Two hours later, I'm on my fourth tumbler and beginning to feel the numbing effects of the whiskey when the door buzzer sounds. I check the peephole and curse under my breath - I can't believe that she had the nerve to come back.

I open the door and walk away from it, plucking my glass off the table and taking a seat on the sofa.

"Jake?" Prue walks in holding a small overnight bag. "I'm sorry I took so long but Mom was really upset." Her eyes fall to the tumbler of whiskey in my hand, "Is everything okay?"

"Was she upset, Prue?" My voice feels flat and my eyes are cold as I look at her. I can see her confusion at my frosty reception.

"Jake, what's wrong? Why are you drinking?"

"Now, there's an interesting question." I can hear the slight slur of my words. "What could possibly drive a man to drink? The answer? A woman! A lying, cheating, deceitful woman."

"Jake, I don't understand..."

"You don't understand, Prue?" I cut her off. "It's me that doesn't understand! I actually thought we had something really special going then, all of a sudden, you leave with some story about your Mom being upset."

"It wasn't *some story*, Jake!"

I hold my hand up, halting her words. "I was worried about you so I got your address from Tyler and came over to make sure you were okay, only to find you weren't there. Your neighbor very kindly told me that you were at the local coffee shop, so I drove over there to find you."

"But, I didn't see you. Why didn't you....?"

"Oh, I know you didn't see me, Prue," I cut across her again. "But, I saw you. In the backseat of your car sticking your tongue down another man's throat!"

"What the hell are you talking about? I don't know what you me...." I see the second it dawns on her, the second she realises she's been rumbled.

"I don't share, Prue. Pick up your little overnight bag and take it and yourself out of my fucking apartment!" My words are coated in ice.

Prue closes her eyes and when she opens them again, I can see the sheen of tears. I harden my heart against the sight even though it rips me up inside to see her cry.

"I see," she whispers. She looks devastated for a minute but then she takes a deep breath and straightens her spine. "I believed you."

I look at her in confusion. "What the hell does that mean?"

"When Kaylee tried to make trouble earlier. I believed you when you said you hadn't been with her. I didn't need you to say it, I already knew it because despite the short amount of time we've spent together I've come to know you, the you that not many people get to see."

Prue dashes away a tear. "Sometimes you can spend your whole life with someone and never really know them. And sometimes, if you're really lucky, you can spend five minutes with someone and feel like you've known them your whole life. That's how it's been for me with you. I'm just sorry that you don't feel that too. When you've had time to calm down and think about things, you might see things more clearly. You know where I am if you do. But I won't wait forever."

She's good. *Really* good. Oscar-worthy. "Close the door on your way out, Prue."

I drain my whiskey glass and watch as she leaves my apartment, and my life, with her head held high.

PRUE

I can hardly see where I'm going through the tears clouding my vision. How did everything go to shit so quickly? This afternoon, I was the happiest I've ever been. Now, everything has come crashing down around me.

If I'm totally honest with myself, I know I should take some of the responsibility. I should have opened up about my past to Jake before now, had planned to do exactly that when I came back to the apartment tonight. I was going to tell him everything, but finding him that way, so cold and closed-off and not even prepared to listen, has put paid to that.

I'm pissed that he was so quick to believe that I would go from his arms to someone else's. I push down the little voice that reminds me how devastated he was at Monica's betrayal, how it destroyed his ability to trust. But he should know I'm not Monica. I'm Prue. The woman who gave herself over to him body and soul. And he's just trampled all over those gifts and thrown them back in my face because of a misunderstanding.

Maybe I should have told him what he'd really seen but my stubborn pride says I shouldn't have to prove my innocence - he either knows it or he doesn't.

As I take the elevator down, I pull out my phone and call Daryl – he wouldn't let me drive myself over earlier, insisting that he bring me. If he's surprised to hear me calling him again so soon, he doesn't let on and promises to come get me straight away.

So much has changed in the space of a few short hours. I thought I'd be sleeping in Jake's arms tonight but I guess it wasn't meant to be.

As I step out of the lift and walk down the corridor toward the exit to wait for Daryl, a weird sensation rolls down my spine and goose-bumps chase down my arms.

A split second later I'm shoved hard from behind and sent sprawling on the concrete, my head bouncing off the hard surface. The force of the impact knocks all the air from my lungs and my head feels as if it's about to explode. The attack has come so suddenly that I'm completely disoriented.

"Hello, Prudence."

I manage to roll onto my back, winded and fighting for breath and look up at a face I haven't seen for almost ten years.

Oh God, he's found me!

He looks different. His head is shaved and the stubble that covered his neck and jaw is now gone, replaced by tattoos. But his eyes have the same sick lust in them that they did back then.

I think there was always a small part of me that knew he would find me, that the nightmare wasn't over.

My eyes drop to his hand and my heart falters when I see the glint of a blade. "How....?" I don't have enough breath to finish the question.

"How did I find you? Easy when you have such helpful neighbors." He smiles at me like a hungry crocodile playing with a tasty morsel right before eating it. "Wasn't difficult to follow you there. I'm a patient man and I knew it would only be a matter of time until you were on your own."

I close my eyes. Poor Mr. Grimes would've had no idea who he was talking to, the information he was giving to a convicted felon.

I feel a warm stickiness over my eye and reach up to touch my head, grimacing as my fingers come away covered in blood.

The world is spinning around me and I'm having trouble focusing. I know I need to get up from my vulnerable position on the ground but I can't seem to make my body obey the commands of my mind.

He licks his lips, much as he did that day in my bedroom and I swallow my nausea. "We have unfinished business, *chica*. I'm here to collect on your daddy's debt. You were asking for a good fucking even then, standing there with your little shorts on like a fucking cock-tease. Your daddy handed me the perfect opportunity to get inside that tight pussy of yours and I've waited years to collect on that debt. You're gonna pay up in full now and after I'm done with you, your whore of a mama's gonna pay too!" Spittle flies from his mouth and he's breathing hard as he walks toward me.

With a superhuman effort, I drag myself to my feet, turning to sprint into the parking lot. I need to get out in the open, find someone, anyone, that can help me.

As I emerge from the corridor into the night air, I see the car with the engine running, and I realize too late that I've just played straight into his hands, that he means to get me in that car and take me God knows where.

I come to an abrupt halt, knowing that I can't allow that to happen. My only choice is to fight but before I have chance to process my next move, his body comes barrelling into me from behind and we both tumble to the ground.

He flips me roughly onto my back, kneeling on the ground as he forces himself between my thighs. "I told you last time not to run from me, *chica*." His saliva sprays me in the face, his eyes bulging with excitement and lust as he wraps his hands around my throat.

Instinct takes over as my years of self-defence training kicks in and an odd sense of calm falls over me. I've learned various choke hold techniques over the last ten years, including how to break them.

I cross my arms and grab both of his wrists with my hands, slamming my elbows down against his arms to break his hold, but he's too strong. I can feel his hands tightening around my throat and I know I don't have much time before he cuts off my oxygen supply completely and I lose consciousness. The thought of what he could do to me if that happens unlocks a reservoir of strength I didn't know I had.

I thrust my hips up off the ground, slamming them back down

again as I curl my upper body into a crunch position, ignoring the pain in my back from the harsh contact with the concrete.

The motion loosens his hands enough for me to drop my chin, gaining some precious air and I wiggle my hips from one side to the other, looping my legs under his arms so that I can slam my feet against his hips, pushing him back and away from me with all the strength I possess.

He grunts as he's forced to release his grip but immediately lashes out at me with his arm. I'm vaguely aware of a painful pressure against my stomach before I thrust out with my feet, unleashing almost ten years-worth of pent-up fury on him. I'm not a little girl anymore and he's never going to put his filthy fucking hands on me again!

My technique isn't pretty but it's effective as I pound into his face, my feet finding their mark as his head snaps back. I kick again and again until blood spurts from his mouth and his nose is a bloody pulp. I kick until his head cracks back one final time and he topples backward from his knees, landing on the ground with a heavy thump.

Adrenaline is still coursing through my system as I jump to my feet and drop into a fighting stance, waiting for him to get up and come at me again but he doesn't move. He's out cold.

The only sound in the still night is my harsh breathing and the pounding of my heart in my ears. It seems like hours have passed since he first shoved me to the ground when in fact it's only been a matter of minutes.

I suddenly become aware of pain all over my body, the worst of it being my stomach. I look down to see blood seeping through my t-shirt and lift the hem to see a wound in my side, steadily oozing blood. Shit! I vaguely remember him striking out at me with his arm. The bastard has stabbed me!

Hysterical laughter bubbles up in my throat. I've managed to fight him off but I'm still going to die by his hand.

No sooner have I thought it than my legs start to give way and blackness creeps in around my peripheral vision. I place my hand over my side and try to stagger back towards the apartment block. I need to get to Jake.

The movement causes a red-hot pain to lance though my body and I lean forward vomiting the contents of my stomach onto the concrete in front of me.

The numbing effects of the adrenaline are wearing off and shock is kicking in as I sink to the cold ground. I know I should get up, try to get help, but I can't seem to make any part of my body cooperate.

My stomach hurts and there's blood on my hands but I can't remember how it got there. My eyes flutter closed and Jake's image is there, behind my eyelids. That's right, I need to get to Jake. Someone's hurt and needs help. Who is it? I don't remember.

My world tilts on its axis as I try again to drag myself up from the ground, crying out with the agony the movement causes.

The sound of a car approaching and the squeal of tires seems to be a million miles away through a dark tunnel.

"Prue? Oh, my God! Prue!"

The voice sounds like my Mom. Why is my Mom here? And why is she so upset?

"Prue! Can you hear me?" A man's voice now, one I vaguely recognise.

I try to answer, tell them that I just need to sleep, that I don't want to get up yet. I just want five more minutes before I have to get ready for school.

This is my last thought as I lose my battle with consciousness.▢

JAKE

The whiskey is barely taking the edge off the pain. I should know by now that losing myself at the bottom of a bottle doesn't solve anything. Been there, got the t-shirt, book and every other fucking piece of merchandise.

Too late, I realise just how much I've allowed what happened with Monica to continue to overshadow the rest of my life, how I've judged Prue by her same shitty standards.

My eyes may have seen one thing but my heart knows something different. Prue wouldn't cheat on me. It's not in her.

I should have stopped her from leaving, at least given her the opportunity to tell me her version of events. If I had, maybe she'd be in my bed now, in my arms, and I would be loving her in every way imaginable.

She was genuinely devastated when I confronted her with what I'd seen but the pain I was feeling at the time had prevented me from seeing the truth of her reaction. There's a version of events that I don't know yet and I just need that last puzzle piece for it all to make sense.

My pity party of one is interrupted by the sound of the door buzzer. Who the fuck is calling on me at this time of night? I frown, debating whether to answer it when the buzzer goes again. Shit!

I walk to the door, checking the peephole, and for a second I think Prue has returned. The woman outside my door looks like Prue, but not.

"Jake! I know you're in there! Open the door, please! It's Prue, she been attacked!"

I throw the door open, instinctively taking a step back as the woman who looks so much like Prue reaches toward me, grabbing my hand.

"My name is Trish Daniels. I'm Prue's Mom. I don't have time to explain, but Prue has been attacked in the parking lot outside. Daryl, my fiancé is with her now and an EMT is on the way. But she's asking for you, Jake."

Time seems to slow as my brain tries to catch up with what Trish is telling me, the fog of the whiskey impeding my ability to think clearly.

"Jake! Focus! Prue needs you."

I notice the blood on Trish's clothing. Prue's blood. She's hurt!

It's all I can do to nod, not trusting my voice as I'm suddenly stone, cold sober. I shove my feet into my sneakers and follow Trish to the elevator, scared of what I'm about to find.

The sight that meets my eyes as we enter the parking lot is like something from a nightmare. Prue is on the ground covered in blood. There's blood coming from her head and the front of her t-shirt is soaked in it.

What the fuck has happened here?

A tall guy with dark hair is leaning over her, putting pressure against a wound on her stomach and my heart falters. Jesus, she's been stabbed!

I drop to my knees at her side, reaching for her cold hand as I lift tortured eyes to the older man who must be Daryl, Trish's fiancé. "Is she....?"

"She's alive," he replies. "Her pulse is thready but the paramedics are on their way."

"On their way? She could be dead by the time they get here!" I shout, my emotions getting the better of me.

"Jake." Prue stirs below me, her fingers twitching against mine.

"I'm here, sweetheart. I'm here!" I lift her hand to my mouth, kissing her icy fingers. I've never felt so fucking helpless in my whole life! "Just hang on, Prue. Help is coming, sweetheart. Don't you leave me, you understand?"

"He found me, Jake!" Her words are a whimper and I have no idea what she's talking about. A strange look passes between Daryl and Trish, one which I'll be questioning later.

"I've restrained the guy who attacked her." Daryl's voice is quiet as he looks behind me and I follow his gaze to a man lying ten feet away on the ground unconscious and handcuffed, his face a bloody mess. I hadn't noticed him earlier, my whole attention focused on Prue.

I look at Daryl. "Prue did that to him?"

Daryl nods. "She went down fighting."

That thought makes me feel a little better, but not much and before I know it I'm on my feet heading toward the unconscious man, intending to do some serious damage to him myself.

Strong arms grasp me from behind. "Don't!"

I must have forty pounds on Daryl but he's a lot stronger than his leaner physique suggests. "Trust me, Jake, I'm a cop and as much as I'm on board with what you want to do, it's not going to help Prue if you or I are arrested for beating the ever-loving crap out of that piece of shit."

Daryl's words stop me in my tracks as I realize where the handcuffs came from and the fight leaves my body.

Daryl releases me and I move back to Prue's side, where Trish is bent over her, tears streaming down her cheeks as she smooths Prue's hair gently back from her face.

I take Prue's hand in mine again as I hear the sound of approaching sirens.

The next hour passes in a blur as the cops and EMT unit arrive. I force myself to move out of the way while the paramedics work on Prue, watching as they load her onto a gurney. I make to follow, but Daryl steps in front of me and puts a hand on my chest.

"Let them do their job, Jake. We can follow them in my car."

I nod, knowing he's right. "Why would he want to hurt Prue? I don't understand."

Daryl gives me a weary look. "Let's get to the hospital and you and Trish can talk there."

Thirty minutes later we're parking at the hospital where they've taken Prue. I call Ty on the way, giving him a brief rundown of events and asking him to head over to lock up my apartment.

Other than my phone call, the car ride over is a silent one with Daryl, Trish and myself lost in our own thoughts, trying to process the events of the last few hours.

We head straight inside and Trish signs the release papers for Prue, who's being prepped for surgery.

Trish turns to me. "Let's go see if we can find the cafeteria and grab a coffee. I could use the caffeine."

A small smile lifts my mouth. Like mother like daughter. God, was it only yesterday that I'd gone to get coffee for Prue? Seems like another life now. I don't usually drink coffee but I could use some caffeine myself right now.

"I'll wait here in case there's any news," Daryl says. "I'll come find you if you're needed." He pulls Trish in for a hug and gives her a lingering kiss, and I feel like I'm intruding on a private moment.

It doesn't take long to find the hospital cafeteria. It's the early hours of the morning so it's relatively quiet. We grab a table and sit facing each other with our coffee.

I get straight to the point. "It's my fault." I see Trish's questioning look. "What happened to Prue. I could have prevented it."

"And how exactly do you think you could have done that, Jake?" Trish looks me directly in the eye.

I find myself telling her everything, from my break up with Monica to meeting Prue to my accusations the previous evening and the sickening realization that it wasn't Prue in the back of the car earlier. It was Trish and Daryl. All I'd seen was the flaming red hair and jumped to what I thought was the only conclusion. The knowledge of how I've fucked up makes me sick to my stomach.

"I should have listened to what Prue had to say, should've known she's not like that. Instead I chose to believe the worst and sent her running straight into danger. Right outside my fucking apartment! Sorry," I add quickly, apologising for my language, but Trish just smiles.

"Believe me, I've heard much worse than that." She leans back in her chair, closing her eyes for a second before continuing. "You're not the only one blaming yourself for this whole mess, Jake. I have a huge part to play in it too." Her voice is full of bitterness. "We were both finally moving on with our lives, and now this!" Her eyes glisten with unshed tears and it seems the most natural thing in the world to reach across and grasp her hand on the table.

She looks at me and gives me a watery smile, squeezing my hand in return. "The reality is that it's no one's fault apart from that bastard who put my daughter in hospital. He had a score to settle and if it wasn't outside your place it would have been somewhere else, Jake. If he'd managed to get her in that car she'd be dead now." Trish's voice breaks and she takes a deep breath, trying to gain control of her emotions.

The thought of Prue lying dead somewhere terrifies me. "Why Prue? What did she ever do to him?"

Trish looks at me for a moment before replying. "Let me ask you a question first, Jake. You love her, don't you?"

I nod. "More than I ever thought possible. But I've fuc...messed up big time," I catch myself, giving Trish an apologetic look but she just waves it away. "I don't know if she'll be able to forgive me."

"I know my daughter better than anyone, Jake, and I'm pretty sure she loves you too. She wouldn't have had sex with you otherwise." Trish's frankness is unexpected and I feel my cheeks heating like a naughty schoolboy. "It's good to know that men can still blush in this day and age," Trish chuckles.

Her eyes fall to her coffee cup and she twirls her spoon absently. "Things were tough for Prue growing up. Her father and I married young and I was already expecting Prue. For a few years things were okay but when Prue was about six-years-old Pete lost his job. Good jobs were hard to come by and he spiralled into a depression. I had to sacrifice a lot of time with Prue to hold down two jobs to keep us above the breadline.

"Our marriage suffered as a result and we just grew further and further apart. Pete would go out for hours at a time and I never really questioned it, was just glad that Prue and I didn't have to deal with his moods and unpredictable behaviour. I think a part of me knew, deep down, that something more was going on but I just didn't want to face facts back then."

My stomach turns over thinking about Trish and a young Prue having to deal with all that.

"I told Pete things had to change, he had to get a job or Prue and I were gone. I should have gotten us out then but, naive fool that I was, I didn't want to give up on Pete, on our marriage. I was raised a certain way and believed that marriage was for keeps, for better and for worse and all that."

Trish swallows, swiping at her tears. "One day, when Prue was thirteen years old, I came home early from work. Thank God, I did, because I found Pete in the corner of the living room, a complete wreck, making no sense. I later found out he was high as a kite on heroin.

"I heard noises upstairs and then Prue screamed out for help. I'll never forget it. She was screaming for her daddy to help her and he was cowering in a corner!" Fresh tears track down Trish's face and I squeeze her hand a little harder, trying to comfort her when all I want to do is break things.

"I grabbed the first thing I could think of, a baseball bat I always kept in the kitchen, just in case I ever needed it. When I got to Prue's bedroom there was a man there. He had her.... up against him with a knife at her back and the other in her underwear and h...he..." Trish stops as she tries to compose herself.

"Oh, Jesus!" I feel the rage surging up through my blood as I listen to the nightmare unfolding, the monster putting his hands on an innocent girl. On Prue!

"There was blood on her neck," Trish's words are barely a whisper, "which I later found out was from where he'd bitten her."

Shit! The scar on her neck. My eyes close on a wave of pain as I remember Prue's odd behavior when I'd seen it, how I'd questioned her about it and how desperate she'd been for me to make love to her.

"I tried to hit him but I wasn't quick enough and he knocked the bat out of my hands and came at me, grabbed me by my hair and put the knife against my throat. I'm sure he would have killed me if Prue hadn't picked up the bat. She swung it with everything she had in her and took him down. She was only thirteen. A girl that age shouldn't have had to go through that."

Trish pauses to take a sip of her coffee. "I called the police and they told us to get out of the house, so Prue and I left, went to Barbara's house. She's a good friend and owns the diner where I worked until recently.

"The cops found a whole stash of drugs at our place – under floorboards, hidden behind the backs of cupboards, and various other places. It had been going on under my nose for years and I never saw it, never knew. What a blind fool I was!" Trish laughs bitterly.

"Turns out, Pete was involved in supplying drugs for some guy who was pretty high up in the chain of things. He'd been skimming off the top and had already been warned once so when the main guy found out it had happened again, he sent one of his men to pay him a visit. To teach Pete a lesson through Prue…" Trish's voice trails off and a tear rolls down her cheek.

"Pete was convicted of possession and distribution of Class A drugs and got a discretionary life sentence. The other guy, Diego Martinez, got ten years for attempted rape and possession of Class C drugs. They couldn't prove he was distributing because the drugs were being kept at our house and they only found ketamine's on him. He was too clever to get caught with any of the heavy stuff."

Trish takes another sip of coffee. "Pete has straightened himself out in prison, gone through a drug rehab program. We always knew Martinez would get out one day but on Saturday morning I had a phone call from Pete telling me that he was already out. He was scared for our safety as he'd heard on the prison grapevine that Martinez had been making threats of revenge before he got out. I tried to call Prue to tell her but couldn't get hold of her so Daryl and I drove down here. I have a key to her apartment so we waited there and I finally caught up with her at your place."

And the rest, as they say, is history, I think bitterly. Shit! What a fucking mess!

I lean my elbows on the table in front of me, raking my hands through my hair as I try to come to terms with everything Trish has told me. I should have killed that fucking monster when I had the chance! The thought of him putting his hands on Prue rips me in half and I want to throw things.

Trish reaches across the table and grabs one of my hands with both of hers, her touch strangely calming. "So, as you can see, you're not the only one who thinks they could have prevented everything that's happened. I've wasted years of my life doing that, torturing myself with the 'what ifs' of every decision I ever made. But you know what, Jake? It doesn't change a damn thing. What's done is done. All we can do is learn from it because if you don't, you just stay locked in the past, which is exactly where I was until I met Daryl. He's shown me that I am worthy of happiness again. Of being loved again. And you are too."

I clear my throat, feeling emotion overwhelm me as I struggle for words. "Thank you for telling me all this, Trish. I wish Prue could have trusted me enough to open up about it all."

"You have to understand the reasons why we had to keep things quiet, Jake. There was a lot at risk, but she and I talked when she came back to her apartment earlier and we agreed that you needed to know. She planned on telling you when she got to your place. Obviously, your misunderstanding got in the way of that."

I feel like the biggest fucking idiot ever and promise myself then and there that I will never jump to hasty conclusions again where Prue is concerned.

"So, what are you going to do, Jake?" I lift my eyes to Trish's, her question catching me off-guard. "Are you going to wallow in self-pity, or are you going to fight for what you want? For what my daughter wants?"

I'm still trying to formulate an answer when I see Daryl walk into the cafeteria. He stops at Trish's side. "Surgeon wants to talk to us, honey."

We're directed to a private room and I hesitate but Trish grabs my hand and pulls me inside with her and Daryl.

We take a seat and a few minutes later the surgeon enters the room. He looks to be in his forties, with a medium build and sandy colored hair. He introduces himself as Dr. Richards and takes a seat opposite, getting straight to the point.

"Prudence has come through surgery well." Trish exhales in relief as she grips Daryl's hand tightly. "The knife penetrated her transverse colon and she lost a lot of blood. Fortunately, the damage was to the right side so we didn't have to perform a proximal colostomy and we were able to simply suture the area."

The surgeon might well be speaking a foreign language for all I know – the only part I understood was that Prue has made it through surgery.

"Prudence also has trauma to her back and neck as well as a concussion from a blow to the head, which we'll need to monitor closely."

Dr. Richards pauses. "Please don't be alarmed if her eyes are bloodshot and she's unable to talk for a few days. This is quite normal after an attempted strangulation."

Normal? There's nothing fucking normal about this whole situation!

I push down my anger at the list of Prue's physical injuries. I can't help but wonder how deep the mental and emotional injuries go but I do know that we'll face them together, whether she likes it or not.

"She's currently in recovery but she'll be moved to a room shortly so you should be able to see her in about an hour. She'll need to stay in for several days, but I'm optimistic at this point that she'll make a full recovery, physically at least."

Dr. Richards voices take on a sympathetic note. "She's been through a traumatic experience and we have highly trained counsellors we can put you in touch with if you wish."

Trish thanks the surgeon as he leaves and we head to the waiting room, surprised to find Tyler there with Jenna curled up against him, half asleep.

They stand as they see us, Ty pulling me in for a rare man-hug, followed by Jenna, who hugs me warmly, her face full of concern. The fact that my friends are here to support me means more than I can say and I quickly dash away the wetness from my eyes.

I introduce them to Trish and Daryl and catch them up with the latest on Prue.

"Oh, thank God!" Jenna's relief is apparent, as she hugs first Trish and then Daryl. "We were so worried!"

"Us too. Guess I raised a fighter - in more ways than one," she smiles weakly.

"She can hold her own in a fight, like her mother," Daryl says, and a look passes between him and Trish.

"Can she have visitors?" Jenna asks.

"We're just waiting for her to be transferred to a room and then we can see her."

"Okay, well Tyler and I are going to head home and get some sleep and let you visit with her now that we know she's going to be okay. We just wanted to come down here ourselves in case there was anything we could do – it seemed better than just waiting around and doing nothing. We'll come back tomorrow to see her." Jenna looks at me. "Jake? Do you need us to take you home?"

"I'm staying." I don't even have to think about my answer. No way am I leaving here. Not until Prue does. I'll sleep in the corridor if I have to.

Tyler and Jenna say their goodbyes and I pull Ty to one side on his way out. "Thanks, man. For everything."

"Anytime." Ty slaps me on the shoulder as he and Jenna leave. "We'll see you tomorrow."

Just over an hour later, we're able to go and see Prue. I hang back, knowing that Trish needs the reassurance of seeing her daughter first. I can wait.

I take a seat at the end of the corridor near Prue's room, resting my head against the wall behind me, fighting exhaustion as the events of the last several hours catch up with me. Now I know Prue is going to be okay, I'll just close my eyes for a few minutes.

I'm woken sometime later with a start as a hand shakes my shoulder. "Sorry to wake you." Daryl looms over me. "Trish thought you'd like some time with Prue." He sits down in the chair next to me. "How you holding up?"

"How I'm holding up isn't important – it's Prue who matters right now. But, thanks for asking."

"Trish filled me in on your conversation. If it's any consolation, you're not the first person to fuck up and you won't be the last." The older man gives me a wry smile. "I seem to remember fucking up pretty good myself when I first met Trish and we both almost paid the ultimate price."

"That sounds like a story I'd like to hear," I say curiously.

Daryl chuckles. "And one I'll be happy to share with you over a cold beer some other time, but for now, get on in there and take care of your woman." Daryl slaps me on the shoulder.

I don't need any further prompting and head back up the corridor to her room.

As I open the door, my eyes fall to Prue's still form in the hospital bed. The white bandage is stark against the dull red of her hair. Her eyes are closed, her face pale and I swallow my rage as I see the red welts and bruising around her neck. She's hooked up to all manner of tubes and devices, some of which are beeping steadily.

"I'll let you have some time alone." My gaze switches to Trish as she rises from the chair next to the bed. "She's gone back to sleep, but it will help her, you just being here. I'm going to go grab another coffee with Daryl, so take your time." She stops in front of me and hugs me unexpectedly. "I like you, Jake." She pats my arm, turns and walks out of the room.

I take the chair that Trish has recently vacated and reach for Prue's hand, watching her eyelids flicker but remain closed, her breathing even.

"I'm not sure if I fell in love with you that night at the party." My voice is husky with emotion. "Maybe that was the start of it.

But whatever that feeling was it pales in comparison to what I feel for you now. It's like comparing a snowflake to a blizzard."

I lean over and gently stroke her hair away from her face. "The feelings I had for Monica pale by comparison. I never really loved her, the pain when we split was bruised pride and a dented ego. I know that now because what I felt for her doesn't come close to what I feel for you. The pain when I let you walk out of my apartment last night turned me inside out."

I lean in and kiss her gently. "You're every fantasy I never knew I had. You've filled empty places in me I wasn't even aware existed."

Prue's eyes open and focus directly on me. "I love you too, Jake." Her voice is a rasp.

I smile at her, placing another gentle kiss against her mouth. "You were listening the whole time, huh?"

"Yep. You're going soft on me."

"Maybe just my heart, but not anywhere else where you're concerned." I grin, gently resting my forehead against hers and sighing as Prue's hands move to tangle in my hair. "I'm so sorry. For everything. For what it's worth, I'd already figured out I was being a complete dick before I even spoke to your Mom - who, by the way, is a pretty amazing woman - like her daughter." I look into Prue's eyes. "I'll never forgive myself for what happened after I sent you away."

Prue strokes my cheek and I turn my head to kiss her palm. "Not all your fault," she croaks. "Should have told you before." Tears leak from her bloodshot eyes, "Was so scared!" My heart twists at the sight of her tears, her poor battered body and I feel her pain like it's my own.

"We don't need to talk about it now. We've got plenty of time for that when you're feeling better. Get some rest, sweetheart."

Prue's hand still grasps mine as if she's afraid to let go. "I'll be here when you wake up, we all will," I assure her and she sighs and closes her eyes.

I sit with Prue and watch the gentle rise and fall of her chest as she sleeps, feeling more content than I ever have in my whole life.

Trish and Daryl return after about an hour and as much as I don't want to leave the hospital, there's something I need to do, something I thought I'd never do again, and I need Daryl's help.

PRUE

When I open my eyes, I have no idea where I am. Then the memories come crashing back and for a few seconds I'm caught in a nightmare again.

"It's okay, honey. I'm here. You're safe now," Mom's voice soothes me and the nightmare recedes. Every inch of me aches and I feel as if I've been hit by a truck.

"Jake?" My voice is a croak. Is he really here? Or did I imagine it all?

"He's stepped out for some fresh air with Daryl, honey. He'll be back soon. How are you feeling? No, don't answer that! Here." Mom hands me a notepad and pen.

Like I've done ten rounds with Mike Tyson, I write.

"You look like it, too," Mom grimaces.

Did they get him?

"They got him, Prue," Mom reassures me. "Along with enough

evidence to put him back behind bars for the rest of his life."

Hearing that goes a long way to allaying my fears. It all seems like a blur to me now, Martinez attacking me and our subsequent fight. I'd tapped into a strength I never knew I had and I still can't quite believe I actually managed to take him down.

"You did a number on his face, Prue," Mom says, as if reading my thoughts. "He was really messed up, by all accounts."

I'll be forever grateful for Mom insisting that we both take self-defence classes when we left our old life behind. Those skills had given me a fighting chance against Martinez - more than that, they had saved my life.

Was determined to kick his ass, or die trying, I scribble.

Mom's eyes fill with tears. "I could have lost you!"

I reach out and squeeze her hand. *Not getting rid of me that easily. My mother is a fighter and I'm my mother's daughter.*

Mom swipes a tear from her cheek. "I love you, Prue."

I love you too, Mom. To the moon and back.

I must fall asleep again because when I wake, Mom is gone and Jake is sitting next to the bed, holding my hand. When he sees I'm awake, he leans over and kisses me softly. "Hello, sleepyhead."

I indicate for him to pass my notepad and pen. *And where do you think you've been?* I give him my best scowl and he chuckles as he reads what I've written.

"There was something I needed to do," Jake chuckles as I raise my eyebrows in question. He sinks down on one knee and my eyebrows shoot into my hairline, my eyes widening, as he produces a small, velvet box.

"I never saw you coming, Prue. You snuck up on my blind side, took the parts of me that were broken and fixed them - in more ways than one." Jake raises an eyebrow and grins at me. "I'm all in, Prue. I'm all in with you, if you'll have me."

Jake opens the box and I can't help my gasp as he reveals a beautiful green gemstone ring, surrounded by diamonds. So, that's what he'd been up to!

"The saleslady said this stone is called peridot and I chose it because it reminds me of your eyes. She also said there's a meaning behind the stone. It means 'I know who you are. I trust you and I love you.' Seemed pretty apt. Will you marry me, Prue?"

Tears roll down my cheeks and splash on the notepad as I write my answer, holding it up so Jake can see.

YES!

Next thing I know, I'm being kissed breathless and wishing I wasn't in this hospital bed so that I can do all the things I want to do to him.

Jake pulls back an inch. "When you're better and have had the all clear from the doctor, I'm going to fuck you senseless until you can't stand up straight and you'll have no choice but to think of me every time you sit down." His breath whispers against my mouth and his promise makes my breath hitch in my throat.

You're such a romantic! I look forward to it! I write, grinning at him.

Jake takes the ring from the box and slides it onto my finger. He grimaces as he sees it's a little big and goes to take it off, but I snatch my hand away, shaking my head. No way is he taking this off now.

He laughs. "Okay, okay! We'll get it resized when we get you out of here."

We're interrupted as Mom pokes her head round the door. "Is it safe to come in?" She asks, grinning. "So? Did you say yes?" She comes fully into the room, her eyes going straight to my ring finger and she jumps up and down like a giddy schoolgirl before hugging Jake and then me. "Congratulations! We can have a double wedding!"

I roll my eyes. Not going to happen.

Daryl comes in behind Mom and shakes Jake's hand before bending to kiss me on the cheek. "Congratulations, kid." He turns to look at Jake. "I have a feeling you're in good hands."

The next few days go by in a blur. I'm still sore and recovering from my ordeal, but each day I feel a little more human again.

The first time I see myself in the mirror, I almost recoil in horror. My body looks like one big bruise and I'm covered in grazes and scratches. The eyes that stare back at me from the mirror are bloodshot and don't even look like mine. My engagement ring certainly isn't a good match at the moment. A large dressing covers the wound on my stomach, making me realize how much worse it could have been if Daryl and Mom hadn't found me when they did.

The police come to take a statement and Daryl sits with me while I tell them everything I remember, down to the finest detail. They reassure me that they have enough evidence on Diego Ramirez to put him back inside for life.

Jenna and Tyler come to visit and Jenna coos over my engagement ring while Tyler just smiles. And as for Jake, he doesn't leave my side for more than a few minutes at a time, using the hospital facilities to wash up and change into the clean clothes that Tyler has brought for him.

A week after I was admitted, I'm finally declared well enough to go home and Jake takes me down to Daryl's car in a wheelchair. Jake gets us settled in the back seat and doesn't let go of my hand the whole ride home.

When we pull up outside my apartment, I notice that not only is my little VW parked outside, but also Jake's Ferrari.

"Tyler brought my car over, along with some clothes," Jake explains. "I'm gonna be your own private nursemaid for a while."

The thought of Jake in a nurse's outfit makes me laugh as he opens the car door and helps me up the path. As I step inside, the safety and familiarity of my apartment washes over me. It's good to be home but I'm exhausted from the car journey.

Mom gets me settled in bed, fussing over me and making sure I'm comfortable before sitting on the edge of the bed next to me. "Daryl and I are going to head back home now you're on the mend, honey. I wish I could stay longer but we both need to get back for work and I'm pretty sure Jake is going to cater to your every whim!" She chuckles.

"I wish you could stay too, Mom, but I understand." My voice is still a little husky but almost back to normal.

Daryl and Mom say their goodbyes, with Mom promising to ring me at least once a day and then Jake and I are finally alone for the first time since the attack.

He comes into the bedroom, carrying a mug of coffee and a plate of cookies, setting the plate down and handing me the coffee where I'm propped up on the pillows.

"You know how to keep me happy," I say, taking a sip from the steaming cup and groaning with pleasure. "That's good! Hospital coffee just doesn't taste the same."

Jake sits next to me on the bed, pulling me gently against him and I'm grateful that he's replaced my double bed with a king size in my absence. His fingers absently play with one of my curls. "I thought it was better if we came back here. I didn't think you'd want to go back to my apartment just yet."

I'm touched by his thoughtfulness and reach up to kiss him softly. "I'm not sure if I'll ever be able to go back, Jake," I admit. "Too much happened there."

"Then we'll find a new apartment. Together."

"You want us to move in together?"

Jake shrugs. "We're getting married, Prue. I want you with me every night between now and then and every night after."

"Wow! That's a lot of nights you're signing up for there. Sure you're up to the job?" I laugh.

"Oh, I'm more than up for the job," Jake growls. "And once you're fully healed, I'll show you exactly how much I'm 'up' for it."

"Promises, promises!" I smile as he kisses me and there's no more talking for quite some time.

4 Weeks Later

JAKE

"I think that's the last of it." Tyler slumps into the chair he's just placed next to the sofa and I hand him a beer.

"Thanks, Ty. Couldn't have done this without your help." I crack the top off my own beer.

"Glad to help. I think you'll be happy here. It's a great place and not far from Jenna and I." Ty salutes me with his beer. "Here's to the future."

It's taken us most of the day but we've finally gotten the apartment ready. It's a little bigger than my old apartment, with a larger kitchen and living area and three bedrooms. Prue and I fell in love with the place and the location as soon as we walked through the door.

My phone vibrates in my pocket and I pull it out to see a text from Prue.

On way. All good. Doc pleased with my progress. Permission to resume normal activities.

There's a smiley face with its tongue sticking out at the end of the message and I nearly drop the phone at the meaning behind her words. Seems like we'll be christening the new apartment in more ways than one tonight.

I'd really wanted to go with Prue today but Jenna had insisted on taking her to her hospital appointment so that Tyler and I could get the apartment ready for her return.

Prue and I have grown even closer over the last month. Despite her recovery going well, she still has nightmares, sometimes waking in the middle of the night screaming and crying. It kills me to see her going through this when all I can do is just hold her and tell her everything is going to be alright.

She's started seeing a counsellor, someone recommended by the hospital, and it's helping her to deal with the trauma of the attack as well as what happened when she was thirteen.

Her recovery has also meant that we've been unable to indulge in anything too physical as I've been worried that it will hurt her. It was at my insistence that we wait to get the go ahead from the doctor and it's damned near killed me.

In fact, we've both been counting the days until she's given the all clear and the thought of being able to bury myself in her soft body again has me turning away and reciting my times tables in my head to hide my reaction from Tyler.

Some shower time is going to be needed to take the edge off before Prue gets home because at this rate I won't be able to last two fucking seconds - and I'll need a lot longer than that

118

for what I've got planned.

"You look happy," Ty says, as I turn back around and I realize I have a shit-eating grin plastered on my face.

"Prue just got the all clear from the doc."

"Ah! I see!" Tyler gives me a knowing smirk and swallows the last of his beer. "In that case, I'll leave you to it."

By the time Prue walks through the door, I'm relaxing on the sofa, having lit the candles, put the champagne on ice and prepared dinner.

"Oh wow! It all looks amazing! You've been a busy boy." She puts her purse on the side table and shrugs off her jacket. "Something smells good. I'm hungry."

"Lasagne and salad. All ready when you are."

Prue slips off her shoes and walks toward me, unbuttoning her jeans and letting them fall down her legs before stepping out of them. Her t-shirt is next until she's standing in front of me in only her lacy white bra and panties. She straddles me where I sit on the couch, looping her arms around my neck and pressing her lace clad pussy against my rigid cock.

"I'm hungry for something else first," she breathes and she reaches behind her to release the catch of her bra, spilling her heavy breasts between us, her nipples already hard little peaks waiting for my hands and mouth.

I groan and cup her tits as my thumbs find her nipples and she arches her back, moaning my name. "I'm on fire for you, Jake. I don't want long and slow. I want fast and hard."

Holy shit, that's hot!

I don't need any further prompting as I strip off my t-shirt and she helps divest me of my jeans and boxers with frenzied hands. My cock stands to turgid attention - jacking off in the shower earlier seems to have done nothing to dampen my need to get inside this woman of mine. And she is mine, every delectable inch of her and in every sense of the word.

I grab her thighs and in one smooth motion, I flip her over so that she's underneath me on the sofa, hooking my thumbs in her panties and tearing them in my haste to get them down her legs.

Prue writhes on the sofa, her beautiful pussy bared to me in all its auburn glory and I want a taste. I press her knees apart, opening her up as I dive between her legs and settle my mouth over her wet folds, giving her one smooth lick from back to front.

Prue cries out and comes up off the couch at the contact of my tongue against her clit and the sound spurs me on, increasing the pressure with every thrust of my tongue against her sensitive nub. She tastes amazing and I could stay here all day eating her juices but already I can feel the spasms of her orgasm overtaking her body. My girl is in a hurry tonight.

I slide my hands up her body to her tits, finding her nipples and giving them a little pinch and she flies over the edge, shouting my name. Fuck, she's noisy. And I love it. Love that I can give her this amount of pleasure.

Before she can come down from her orgasm, I sit up and grip her hips, pulling her toward me so that her ass comes to the edge of the sofa and impale her with one smooth thrust of my hips. We both cry out at the sensation of my cock inside her again, the feeling indescribable. I can already feel my own orgasm building at the back of my balls, the electric shocks travelling up and down my spine.

I look down as I pump in and out of her wet hole, my thumb finding the hard nub of her clit as I drive into her.

"I can't," Prue gasps. "It's too much!"

"You can and you will, sweetheart. Cum for me again. I want to feel your juices all over my cock."

She moans at my words and I feel the contractions of her tight channel, sucking me deep as her climax builds again.

"Oh, my God, oh my God! Jake!" She shouts my name, her juices bathing my shaft as she cums. I follow right behind her, grinding my teeth with the force of my ejaculation, trying to get deeper, closer, as I unload my seed inside her until there's too much for her to hold and it spills out between us.

We collapse in a spent heap against the sofa and I try to catch my breath after the most amazing experience of my life.

Fuck, who am I kidding, every time with her is amazing.

I feel her hands stroking through my hair as I rest my head against her soft breasts, flicking my tongue lazily over a nipple and making her catch her breath again.

"I'll never get enough of you, Prue," I say, pulling her to her feet and lifting her into my arms, carrying her through to the bedroom and lowering her gently to the bed. "We've christened the new sofa, now it's the bed's turn. Don't move."

I head back to the living room and grab the ice bucket with the champagne and take it back to the bedroom. Prue is sprawled out on the bed and the sight of her feeds my soul. She's the most beautiful woman I've ever known and having her in my life has become as necessary as breathing.

I place the ice bucket on the bedside cabinet and take out the bottle of champagne, making Prue giggle as the cork flies toward the ceiling when I open it.

"We need glasses,"

"Not for what I'm going to do." I tip some of the cold champagne over her tits and stomach, making her squeal as the cold liquid hits her skin.

Placing the bottle down I crawl up her body, licking the champagne as I go. I swirl my tongue between the valley of her tits and around her nipples, nipping her gently with my teeth as I go and making her squirm and moan.

Slowly, I move down her soft stomach, lavishing every swell and curve with my mouth and lips, dipping my tongue into her belly button and sipping away the champagne that has pooled there. I reach up and lace my fingers with hers as I gently kiss the scar on her stomach, now a fading pink line.

Her hands pull against mine as she tugs me back up, pushing me gently so that I roll onto my back as she straddles my thighs.

Reaching over, Prue takes a mouthful of champagne and bends to take my cock in her mouth. The combination of the cold champagne, the fizz of the bubbles and her warm lips has me arching off the bed, pushing my cock further into her mouth, the movement causing some of the champagne to leak out.

She releases my swollen shaft, swallows the champagne and proceeds to lick the remaining drops from around my balls, finding numerous sensitive spots that make me feel as if I'm going to combust.

"Pass me an ice cube," I growl and she plucks one from the ice bin, running it up my abs and making me groan, before I'm able to wrestle it from her.

I trail the ice cube across her collar bones and between her tits, drawing little circles on her skin as I move closer and closer to her nipples. She moans and shivers as I circle each tight peak with the ice, trailing it down her stomach and between her legs, pressing it against her clit at the exact moment I thrust up into her.

I position her so that the ice cube is held in place between our bodies as we find a rhythm, our breathing ragged and her moans becoming louder and louder as the ice cube melts against her clit with each thrust of my hips.

Prue grinds against me as she climbs her orgasm, her knees pressing into the mattress and her thighs gripping my hips as she rides me until her back arches and her body vibrates with the strength of her climax.

"Oh God, Prue!" I feel my body empty into hers as we cum together, our bodies straining and sweating against each other as we try to cling to the last silvery tendrils of pleasure.

Prue collapses against me, the only sound that of our labored breathing.

Later, we take a shower, our hands lingering as we soap each other. I can't seem to stop touching her, even though our passion is spent - for now.

After we've dried, we quickly dress and I rescue the lasagne from the oven, where it's been keeping warm. We're both starving and make short work of the meal by candlelight, smiling at each other as we enjoy a glass of the champagne to celebrate our first evening in our new home.

I can see Prue's eyes beginning to droop as we finish our meal – she still tires easily even though her recovery has been smooth and I've just worn her out in the most delectable way possible.

"Come on, woman. Let's get you to bed." I pull her from the chair and lead her back to the bedroom.

We undress and climb into bed, Prue curling up against me, throwing her leg over mine as she rests her head on my chest. I trail my fingers over her soft skin, lingering on the scar at her neck and she stiffens.

"Do they ever bother you? My scars?" Prue asks, an edge of uncertainty in her voice, as her hand roams over my chest.

I think for a minute before answering. "I couldn't give a shit about the scars themselves, if that's what you mean. I love you regardless of any flaws you think you have. The only thing that bothers me is the pain you went through getting them."

Prue sighs. "The scar on my stomach I can live with," she grimaces at the irony of her statement, "because although he inflicted it, he did it with an inanimate object. The scar on my neck bothers me more because it's a constant reminder of his mouth on me when he bit me. That it left a permanent mark on me and I can't ever wash it off." She releases a shaky breath, obviously fighting off old nightmares.

I wind my hands through her hair, tipping her head back so she's looking at me. "I seem to remember a certain person telling me that the past only has the power to hurt us if we let it," I say, referring to the morning in my apartment after Kaylee had paid a little visit.

"I know, Jake. But saying the words and living them are two different things. How do you let go of the pain? The memories?"

"A day at a time, sweetheart," I say. "When you were in the hospital, and I was giving myself a hard time about everything that had happened, your Mom gave me a piece of advice that I'll never forget. She told me that we can't change what's happened in the past, but we can choose if we become a prisoner of it."

"This," I feather my fingers over the scar at her neck, "and this," I trace the scar on her stomach, "are the battle scars of what you survived, no more, no less. Physical scars will heal and the emotional ones only have the power to hurt you if you continue to let them." I wipe the tears from her eyes with my thumbs. "I've got another sixty years or so to keep reminding you, as often as you want to hear it, how much I love you exactly the way you are, scars and all."

Prue pulls my head down for a soft kiss. "Thank you," she breathes against my lips before snuggling back into my side.

"You remember back in the hospital, how you said you fell for me the night of the party?" She waits for my nod. "It was like that for me too. One kiss and you broke down all the walls I'd put up. I didn't want to risk letting a man hurt me again, any man, but there was something about you and I didn't want to run anymore." She chuckles, "Who'd have thought that Marilyn Monroe and Shrek would be such a good match?"

"Now there's an idea for a role play," I leer at her. "You put that sexy little number back on and I'll throw you over my shoulder and carry you back to my swamp and smear you with mud."

Prue throws her head back and laughs and the sound washes over me, fills me up. "Kinky! You sound like the guy from the date I went on that time."

I raise my eyebrows. "Then let's go find some feathers and a banana!"

Six Months Later
PRUE

"You look amazing!" Jenna stands back so she can check me over one last time. "Absolutely stunning," She declares. "Just how every bride should look on her wedding day."

My wedding dress is white and modelled loosely on the iconic Marilyn Monroe dress that I wore the night of the fancy dress party, the night Jake and I first met. It has a fuller, longer skirt which reaches the floor in drapes of silk and the plunging neckline is decorated with a lace insert and pearls, providing a sexy yet modest look and keeping everything in place. No way do I want my girls popping out on my wedding day!

My hair is swept up and secured with pearl pins, some of my red curls left loose around my face to soften the look. My makeup is subtle but brings out the green of my eyes and the soft pink of my lips and I've never felt more beautiful.

Jenna looks stunning in her simple, floor length emerald green bridesmaid dress which clings to her lithe figure and matches her dark colouring perfectly.

"Are you ready, honey?" Mom is wearing a cream two-piece skirt suit, her hair in an elegant chignon beneath her matching hat, and I've never seen her look lovelier. She has an inner glow about her these days, a happiness that shines through her eyes. She's my first and only choice to walk me down the aisle and give me away at the intimate ceremony Jake and I have chosen.

I take a deep breath, a swarm of butterflies going crazy in my stomach. "More than ready, Mom. Time to make that man mine," I grin.

"He's already yours, Prue," Mom replies, softly. "Has been since he first laid eyes on you."

Her words make my eyes well up with tears and I flap my hands in front of them. "Don't make me cry. I'll spoil my makeup!"

Mom hands me my bouquet and loops her arm through mine. "I think we'll both be needing a touch up to our makeup before the day is done."

As neither Jake nor I have religious backgrounds, we decided to opt for a civil ceremony and hired a function room and bar at a swanky hotel. The wedding itself is taking place outside in the gardens and all the chairs and decorations have been laid out for our guests, which include many of Jake and Tyler's teammates as well as friends and colleagues from the clinic where Jenna and I work.

Jenna, Mom and I take our positions behind the doors that will open to reveal the gardens, guests, and of course, my soon-to-be-husband.

A sudden thought occurs to me just as the music starts up and I turn to my Mom in panic. "Mom, you don't think Jake would dare come as Shrek, do you?"

My question comes too late and Mom is unable to answer as the doors open……

An hour later, the justice of the peace announces that we are husband and wife and Jake bends me back over his arm as he kisses me deeply and thoroughly, finally letting me up for air to the whistles and cheers of our guests.

My panic was immediately chased away when I saw Jake waiting for me looking utterly gorgeous in his wedding suit, tailored to mould every muscle in his body, and it was all I could do not to ravish him there and then in front of all our guests. Which wouldn't have been the best idea.

The rest of the day passes in a blur of eating, drinking, dancing and celebrating and by the time midnight arrives, I'm running on fumes.

Mom and Daryl, and Jenna and Tyler are staying at the hotel tonight along with some of the other guests, but Jake and I have booked a cab to take us back to our apartment, as we're leaving early tomorrow morning for our honeymoon in France.

Just as we're getting ready to leave, Jenna pulls me to one side, beaming from ear to ear and holding up her ring finger, showing off a beautiful solitaire diamond engagement ring.

"Ty just asked me to marry him," she says excitedly. "We went back to our room for a…uh…that is…um...for a rest, and he asked me!" Jenna's face gets redder and redder as she talks, making me laugh.

"I'm so happy for you!" I pull her to me and hug her tightly, doing the same to Tyler as he appears behind her. "Did you know about this?" I ask, turning to look at Jake.

"Ty may have mentioned that tonight was the night," Jake replies, hugging Jenna and slapping Tyler on the shoulder.

"Everyone is getting married!" I say excitedly. "Mom and Daryl in a few months and now you and Tyler."

"Babies next!" Jenna jokes and both Tyler and Jake's faces pale.

It's almost one in the morning by the time Jake and I arrive back at our apartment and I giggle as Jake swings me up in his arms, carrying me over the threshold.

He kicks the door shut and strides toward the bedroom, lowering me gently to the floor. His eyes lock on mine, elevating my heart rate and making my stomach swirl with anticipation.

"You look absolutely stunning today, Mrs Matthews. Like a dream come true walking down that aisle towards me." He pulls me to him and kisses me, making me moan as my mouth opens to the invasion of his tongue.

"You took my breath away, too," I whisper against his lips. "I panicked just before I came out with Mom, thinking you might have come dressed as Shrek."

Jake's laugh rumbles against my chest. "I'm pretty sure you wouldn't have married me if I'd done that."

"I would have married you if you'd worn a fig leaf and a smile!"

"Fig leaves, feathers – I can't keep up!" Jake grins, backing me up toward the bed.

"Wait!" I put my hands against his chest, halting him in his tracks. "Take a seat on the bed. I have a wedding gift for you to unwrap."

"You're the only gift I want to unwrap right now," Jake growls, reaching for me again, but I move toward the bathroom.

"Sit. I'll be back in a minute."

I quickly step out of my dress and underwear, hanging the dress up on the back of the door. My curls tumble down my back as I remove the pins from my hair and I slip on a silky, black negligee before retrieving Jake's gift from where I hid it in the bathroom cabinet.

Jakes eyes widen and his mouth drops open as I walk back into the bedroom.

"Woman, you are going to be the death of me," he groans, his eyes raking up and down my body like hands, making my nipples harden in anticipation.

I stop in front of him where he's sitting on the edge of the bed,

slapping his hands away as he tries to reach for me. "Ah, ah! First things first." I hand him the box, wrapped in silver paper with green ribbon. My heart is trying to escape from my throat because I'm not sure what Jake's reaction is going to be.

I slide the straps of my negligee from my shoulders and it pools at my feet at the same time Jake pulls the wrapping paper away and lifts the pregnancy test from the box inside.

His eyes shoot to mine in shock as I stand in front of him, completely naked, before moving to my breasts, which are fuller and heavier, and down to my stomach.

My nervousness increases as the silence stretches on and I'm about to start really panicking when Jakes pulls me to him and buries his mouth against my stomach, kissing me there gently, almost reverently. He lifts his eyes to mine and I see the sheen of emotion in them.

"I know we never actually discussed it," I say, nervously, "but we haven't been using anything so I guess it was only a matter of time."

Jake stands and pulls me into his arms, holding me so tightly that I can barely catch my breath. "How long?" His voice is thick with emotion.

"Early days. About ten weeks. I've known for a few weeks but wanted to surprise you today, on our wedding day. Are you…are you happy?"

"Happy? Happy doesn't cover it, sweetheart! I never thought…" he pauses, trying to compose himself, "I never thought I would be this lucky."

"Thank God! I was so nervous! I didn't know how you'd feel about a baby after what happened with……"

Jake places his fingers over my lips, stilling my words. "That was another lifetime ago, before I met you. You taught me what real love is, Prue, and just when I think I can't love you any more than I already do, I fall in love with you just a little bit more."

"That makes two of us," I whisper, my eyes filling with tears as I pull his head down to mine for a kiss. He pulls away suddenly.

"Is it safe for us to….?"

"Perfectly safe," I reassure him and it's all the encouragement he needs as he gently places me on the bed and proceeds to take his clothes off, giving me a show as he does so, baring his perfect body to my eager eyes. "Hurry!" I moan, writhing on the bed, wanting the feel of him against me, inside me.

He lowers himself on the bed next to me and I reach for him, but he takes my wrists in one of his hands and stretches my arms above my head, holding them there. "No touching, Prue. Not until I say so, okay?"

His words turn me on even more and I nod, nearly cumming right then as he dips his head to my breast and pulls a nipple into his mouth, stroking it with his tongue before turning his attention to the other one.

His mouth moves down my body, leaving a trail of fire behind it as he licks, sucks and nibbles my skin. My body is so attuned to him now that my reactions are instant, anticipating the pleasure to come.

He pauses at my stomach, cupping the tiny swell with his hand as he kisses me there, before moving down to my moist centre and spreading me open to claim me with his lips and tongue. I arch against his mouth, drowning in the pleasure he's giving me, but I want more. I want to touch him.

"Jake, please!"

"Okay, sweetheart." He moves back up my body, kissing me deeply so that I can taste myself on his lips.

"I adore you," I breathe against his mouth, smiling as I open my legs, wrapping them around his hips and pulling him to me so that the tip of his swollen shaft is against my slickness, tempting him inside. "Show me how much you love me," I demand, kissing him and pulling his bottom lip inside my mouth, biting gently and causing him to moan as he slowly, slowly merges his body with mine, giving me an inch at a time until he's buried to the hilt.

"I could stay like this forever," he whispers as he begins to pump his hips in smooth motions, his mouth dipping to my breasts again and suckling my sensitive nipples, making me moan and clench my muscles around him.

"Hard, Jake," I demand, "Fuck me hard!" He loves it when I talk dirty.

"The baby," he gasps.

"The baby is fine, Jake. Nothing we do will harm him."

"Him?"

"It's got to be a boy," I moan, moving with him as he thrusts in and out of my body "with your dark hair and chocolate eyes."

"Jesus, Prue! Do you know how fucking sexy it is, knowing that our baby is growing in here?" He touches my stomach lovingly.

"Show me how sexy," I dare him, biting his shoulder.

Jake growls and moves his hand down, finding my clit with his thumb and rubbing back and forth over the sensitive nub, making me gasp and moan as I feel my orgasm approaching.

I grip his ass and hold him against me, spreading my legs wider and opening myself up to him more deeply as he loses control and drives himself against me.

"That's right, baby. Hard and fast," I gasp in his ear. "It's our wedding day and want us to cum together!"

He moves his hand up to my mouth and I suck my juices from his thumb as our bodies slap together in a frantic rhythm, faster and faster until we both explode.

"Jake!" I scream his name as my climax buffets me, stronger than anything I've felt before, thanks to the pregnancy hormones flooding my body. On and on it goes and as I hear Jake shout his orgasm above me, it sends me over the edge again. My body is drawn as tight as a bow as I spasm over and over in a never-ending surge of ecstasy that eventually leaves me exhausted and boneless with pleasure.

"Wow! That was……"

"Fucking awesome!" Jake finishes, and we both laugh, still trying to catch our breath.

When I can walk again, I quickly clean myself up in the bathroom, climbing back into bed and snuggling up against Jake as he pulls me to him, one hand resting against my stomach.

"Love you, husband."

"Love you more, wife."

I sigh and close my eyes, my nightmares of the past replaced with dreams of the future.

Read on for an excerpt from Playing Deep – Tyler and Jenna's story and Book 1 of the Play Series.

TYLER

I park the Harley, cut the engine and remove my helmet, still straddling the bike.

My eyes wander to the front of the church and I grimace as the memories bombard me. It's been years. Too many and not enough. The pain is still there, burning like an acid in my stomach and a cancer in my brain.

Every Sunday morning my father would drag me here so he could spout his three Hail Mary's and repent his sins before we returned to our shitty life.

Fucking hypocrite.

I run my finger under the collar of my shirt. I hate suits and it doesn't feel right to be wearing one on the Harley. A Harley is meant for jeans and leathers.

A movement captures my gaze and I see her as she walks into the church with her father. She's the reason I'm here….and the reason I left in the first place.

Her long, dark hair is swept up into some fancy do, exposing the delicate sweep of her neck and jaw. Her dark brown eyes and pretty lips are seared into my brain. My cock springs to life as I remember those lips on mine - our first kiss had very nearly become our first time and the heat of those memories still has the power to bring me to my knees.

I take in her long legs and the shape of her exquisite ass in the form fitting skirt suit. Just looking at her from a distance gets me hard and I'm already imagining the things I'd like to do to her…with her.

She's always had this effect on me - she just never knew it.

Until one night five years ago. And then I left - without so much as a goodbye or even a note.

Five long years I've stayed away, giving her time to grow up and have the chance to make her own choices - even if those choices don't include me.

Five years spent running away from my feelings. I couldn't let her know back then - she deserved so much more than I could give her. She was too young and I was too fucked up. Maybe I still am.

I had to be here today. The day that she's burying her mother. It won't be easy - I'm pretty sure she hates me for leaving. But I'm back now.

Back to claim what's mine.

JENNA

The church is full of people who've come to pay their respects, a testament to the kind hearted and generous woman my Mom was.

The brain haemorrhage that robbed her of life so suddenly has taken her from us far too soon. Every death of a loved one is too soon. Our hearts are broken and our lives changed forever but I'm grateful that it was quick for her - that she didn't suffer.

I glance at my Dad who sits next to me at the front of the church, his face composed but pale. Mom's body lies just feet away in the oak coffin with a single red rose laid upon the top that Dad gently placed there earlier. His heart must be breaking in two - he's lost the woman he loved. His friend. His Wife. His lover.

My mouth lifts in a bitter little smile. I'd once thought I could have what they'd had together but that dream had also died a sudden death five years ago.

I'm lost in my grief as the priest begins the service. Words and hymns are a dull hum to my ears as tears spill down my cheeks and I say a silent goodbye to my Mom. Dad's own tears leave silvery streaks on his face and he reaches for my hand. He's not an overly demonstrative man so the physical contact is all the more poignant.

After the service, we file outside and her body is lowered into the ground to rest next to my grandparents. The priest says a few more words and I step forward, gently tossing another rose on top of her coffin to join the first.

Dad and I receive the condolences of fellow mourners in a blur of hugs and handshakes as people drift away, back to their own lives.

"I'll go get the car," Dad says.

"Okay. I'll just be a few minutes." My gaze is drawn back to the fresh earth covering the coffin at my feet.

Dad nods. "Take as long as you need."

I sink to the ground as the tears fall freely again.

"I always hated seeing you cry."

The familiarity of the deep timbre has my head snapping up, shock and disbelief sliding through my veins.

"Tyler?"

God, I hate how broken my voice sounds as his name escapes my lips. I'm torn between throwing myself into his arms or kneeing him in his soft and dangly parts.

He looks amazing. He's a beast of a man now, all broad shoulders and overwhelming masculinity in a sharp gray suit - a far cry from the boy I first met with a black eye and a split lip.

Feeling at a disadvantage, I rise to my feet, smoothing my skirt down with shaking hands. He's even taller than I remember and towers over me despite the heels I'm wearing.

His blond hair is neatly styled, replacing the over-long, careless way he used to wear it. My fingers itch as I recall what it was like to run my fingers through that hair, how his mouth felt on mine after so many years of loving him silently.

A spiral of desire unfurls in my lower belly and lands between my legs as the memories of the last time we were together assault me.

I clench my teeth and school my features to hide my weakness. I'm loath to admit that deep down, there is a part of me that has yearned for him today, on the day that my Mom has been put in the ground.

We've always there for each other - since I was ten and he was twelve.

And then five years ago he just up and left without a word. I'm trying to hold onto the pain and anger that thought brings.

"Why the hell are *you* here?" It's more of a statement than a question. I very rarely curse and the fact that I do so now shows how off balance I am.

I'm unprepared for his answer as his blue eyes bore into mine.

"I came back for you".

Printed in Great Britain
by Amazon